THE ~~UN~~MARRIED WIFE

DEDICATION

If I had been perfect, if life had been perfect, if perfection even existed, I would not have been where I am today. Because of you, I am a better version of me. You are my firstborn and with your father having deserted, maybe my only child. Thank you for staying strong all these years of craziness.

A special dedication goes to the inspiration behind this book, the man himself, the Legend Keeper, John.

Email: admin@alianamarshall.co.za
Visit our website: www.alianamarshall.co.za

THE ~~UN~~MARRIED WIFE

CONTENTS

FOREWORD

Interestingly enough, I have always thought about such a book. It is one of those fantasies turned real turned fantasy writing. The content is deep and personal but the wit at which it is presented sure deserves a round of applause.

Because society has stereotyped people so much that it has become a sin to portray one's belief and values in life, this was a very brave and bold step taken by the author. Although there are bits and pieces of fiction, I believe the book portrayed a definite form of reality.

Sussy Marshall

Email: admin@alianamarshall.co.za
Visit our website: www.alianamarshall.co.za

THE ~~UN~~MARRIED WIFE

Preface

In the midst of everything, a lot of people had opinions and believed that they knew me better than anyone. As a matter of fact, I have been called many names by people who never understood what was going on in my life and those who were close, pretended to understand.

Because some things cannot be said out loud in this so-called "normal" world, it is better to put pen in paper to express how one views life. I acknowledge that some people may not be comfortable with the content of this book, but then, everybody has a choice in life. As John used to put it; "every decision you ever make is the right one at that point in time. The hard part is accepting the consequences of all the decisions you make if they do not turn out to favour your perceived outcome. I do not have any regrets in life, I just have life lessons. Being not-normal is my normalcy".

Aliana Marshall

Email: admin@alianamarshall.co.za

Go to our website: www.alianamarshall.co.za

Introduction

This book is not intended to portray any real-life events that may or may not have occurred or give advice on how anyone should live their lives. It is not a book about life; it is a book about a particular life.

The author reserves the right to hold the content of this book as is even if there may or may not be any objections to the content or event purported.

The author shall in no way be held accountable for any hurt or injury that may or may not be perceived to have been perpetuated by the content of this book.

Email: admin@alianamarshall.co.za

Visit our website: www.alianamarshall.co.za

Chapter 1
Prelude

I am half awake and half asleep. The smart people call this state "the hypnagogic state". Some refer to it as hypnagogic hallucinations. Scientists describe it to us less educated people as the experience of the transitional state from wakefulness to sleep. They say mental phenomena that may occur during this threshold consciousness phase include hallucinations, lucid thoughts, lucid dreaming, and sleep paralysis. Whatever that state is, I am in it. I fell into it just after I had said something on the phone. I was on the phone with John's Sister. Because I cannot think straight right now, I have a slight feeling that I could have been on the phone with John himself. I seldom ever talk to his sister these days, so it could not have been her. It was John or maybe not. I do not know. I cannot recall. I am in a hypnagogic state. I am half asleep, half awake. I see people around me. I see my daughter is staring down at me. I try to say something, but the words could not come out. I see white. I see blurry white. The light fades. I am fading with it. The noise is slowly subsiding. I feed cold in my feet. The coldness also subsides. I cannot feel a thing. My hand is stretched over my abdominal area as if I am feeling for something. I cannot recall anything. I fade away.

Suddenly, it is silence. There is no sound or noise from anywhere. I am finally at peace. I cannot feel a thing, not even my own heartbeat. Everything stops. I am gone.

THE ~~UN~~MARRIED WIFE

The Beginning

They say promises are made to be broken. Maybe they are right or maybe they are wrong. Everything is contextual. Everything human beings ever say or do is relative. It is always about something in relation to something else. It is just like the importance of being a good man. There would never be any good men if there were no evil ones. Life itself is a relative phenomenon. Without death, life would not exist. Without darkness, light would also not exist. There is always the importance of making people understand that all their decisions are decisions that have already been made for them, by nature. Unfortunately, as humans are only the messengers, they cannot ever fully grasp the gift of seeing into the future. They could not fully understand the consequences of their decisions. Only nature knows the end results. For humans, all they have to do is to live their lives the best way they know how. They must live life to the fullest. They must understand that people say or do whatever they want because of how it makes them feel.

A good friend of mine once told me that "nobody ever does anything for someone else unless they are benefiting from it themselves. It is always about them. It is always about the doer". At first, I never understood what she meant until one day she had to break it down to me. I am definitely not the cum-laude material so I do not expect people to presume that I should just read between the lines. I am one of those people academics would describe as having "humble education".

It is education, but I am definitely not one who can be referred to as an academic. My friend would try and explain it to me in simpler terms. As she would put it, "in every decision a person makes, the only determining factor is how it will make them feel".

In essence, she was trying to explain to me how selfish people are in this crazy world we live in. Although some perceive selfishness as a bad thing, the truth is, I think it is actually one of the best decision-determiners our Creator has ever given us. Ever wondered how much you would have done in life if it was never about how it would make you feel. As a child, you first learn to walk not to impress your parents or your peers, but it makes you feel all grown up. You wish you could walk all day and all night long. When you start talking, it is the same thing. You would say whatever you want even if it does not make sense to anyone. To you, it would mean the world. You would be thinking that finally, you are part of the squad. You can converse with people around you only to grow up and realize that it was just a self-satisfaction drive that drove you to wanting to learn more. That is one of the reasons why you would play along too when you had your own kids. You would pretend as if you understand them. You would even make a conversation with whatever you think they are trying to say. In all instances, it would still remain; it would be about how it makes you feel.

My friend asked me if I have ever met anyone who did something just for the sake of the other person.

I thought of many examples. I even recalled all the coins I have given people begging on the streets, the food I have bought for that kid at a supermarket once or that time I ended up standing all the way on a thousand-kilometer trip train just because I had to give my seat to that old lady. As I was about to make my bold statement to my friend; that I have done a lot of things just for someone else which did not benefit me in anyway, she followed up her strange question with her version of the response. She told me point blank that even if I think I have done something good just for another person, I was wrong.

The decision I made had nothing to do with the other person but everything to do with me; or should I say, the inner self. It was always about how it would make me feel, what desire it will fulfil and what character would the people around me perceive me as.

It all made sense. It made me really think that, in this world, it is always about you first. Everything you do is because of how you perceive its outcome would make you feel, how people around you would think of you and what desire it would fulfil. It is a clear portrayal of selfishness. I am not in any way saying that selfishness is good because society describes selfishness only at its extreme. When one cares for no one but themselves, only then they perceive them as being selfish. While doing that, they themselves are not aware that the selfish bug in them is the one talking.

Just because they do not feel comfortable with how one carries themselves, then they think it is correct and justifiable for them to dictate how one should behave.

It is all subjective. It depends on how one looks at it and it is mostly a reflectionary action of one's own inner demon.

People talk about commitment, yet they again advocate for moving on. They will tell you to be committed to what you believe in but then turn around and try to convince you to leave if they think whatever you are doing is not working for you. They do not even attempt to see things from your perspective. They just believe that they are your inner voice; they have a right to dictate to you how to live your life.

Come to think of it, this dictatorship is prevalent in every corner of the world and in every situation we encounter. Take your childhood sport for instance. I remember when I was at primary school when my teacher tried to force me to join the school's netball team. I was a total disaster.

I knew that myself but every time I tried to explain, I was told that, "No Aliana, you are just not committed enough". Deep down in my deepest vein, I knew netball was not for me. I was more of a football person, but no, my teacher believed otherwise.

After my teacher realized that keeping me in the team was not doing any good for the entire team, it was actually doing more bad than good, she precipitously told me that "you know Aliana, sometimes some things are just not meant for some people". To my surprise, the preaching of commitment had suddenly changed. It was no longer about commitment. I suddenly did not have to commit to something that I knew very well I was not good at. The world we live in can be contradictory on many aspects. When one commits to something while other people believe that the commitment is misguided, they try and convince them out of it.

I am no way any closer to being a researcher, but I have sure seen a lot of relationships fail because of people outside those relationships. People would want to define how the relationship should be while they themselves are not doing any better, according to my standards. Yet they will work tirelessly trying to end someone's relationship just because they think it is not right, according to their standards.

This is where I am now, I made a commitment. I have made a commitment not to anyone, but to myself and my guardian spirits. Everyone has them. Some people call them their Guardian Angels, some refer to them as their Ancestors and others refer to them as whatever they want but it is still the same thing. It is that inner voice and inner guard who protects and guides you through life. I made a commitment that I will be the best mother I can ever be, the best wife to my husband, the best sister, the best friend and the best in whatever I do.

Somehow some people think it is applaudable to commit to one's course but yet idiotic to commit to a person.

I have been to hell and back and back to hell with him.

I have been loved, hated, humiliated, worshiped, appreciated, despised, and every other thing and feeling you may think of. Yet I am still here. He used to remind me that I broke up with him dozen times and he had always said that he would only do it once. I also have reminded him of how many times I had fights with him because he could not keep it in his pants. We always said; we were our own version of Bonny and Clyde.

He is a good person. He knows that too. He believes that he has a dark heart, but for us who know him "intimately", we can proudly say that he has one of the kindest hearts in the world. He just prefers to appear as a bad person. I guess maybe it is just his ego overshadowing his kindness.

He is a good father, a good brother, a good son, a good grandson and good partner but he has always said "I may be good in a lot of things, and I will try to be but one thing I can never be good at is being a husband". Technically, I should have known that he never intended to get married, but yet, blinded by love, it never crossed my mind. I had made up my mind; I had planned my whole life, or what was left of it, around him. This is the person who accepted me for who I was and who I am. He never judged me in anyway. Instead, I could swear it turned him on because no matter how upset he was, the Legend would never fall asleep when we were together.

I told myself that I would change him. I would make him fall in love with the idea of getting married, having kids and living happily ever after.

Once again, blinded by love, I never really worried about how he had always explained how he pictured his life. It had always been about progress. To him, life was simple.

It was about going to school, getting a job, building a big house, and living a comfortable life. Not at once he ever mentioned the living marriedly happily ever after. What I was certain of is that I would still be in his life, no matter how it turned out.

He likes me. I know that. Sometimes I think he loves me but then I can never know because he says love is a feeling like any other feeling. It comes and goes, and people need to accept that. Just like any other feeling, be it joy, anger, hunger, happiness, or whatsoever feeling, it comes and goes. He always said that what is important is to be content with whoever you are with. One should be able to live with all their versions of themselves, then maybe, you can say you are in a happily ever after relationship.

Our relationship had never been a normal one in any way. He said at first, he was in love with me, and I was not. Then he stopped loving me and I did not even see it. When I started loving him, he was only there to prove a point. I was like a project to him. He had given himself a goal to archive and he was not going to fail at it. Meanwhile, as time went by, I fell in love with him. By that time, clearly, as I would later find out, he was no longer there. He had emotionally moved on. Me being me also, I was determined not to fail. I was determined to prove to myself that I can have a normal relationship.

I must admit, we were from different worlds. How we carried ourselves was chop and cheese. He was a reserved but determined type. He never spoke much, and he never had many friends. He actually believed that the less people who talked to him, the better. While me on the other side, I was everybody's friend. I was that girl that would shout the loudest in the room. Everybody liked me and I liked them back. That is until he showed me things I was never aware of. He showed me what types of people I had surrounded myself with.

If they were male, they had one goal in mind, to get between my legs someday and if they were female, they were there to get to know my life so they could gossip about me.

At first, it did not bother me, but as time went by and as people started showing me their true colours, everything just made sense. I never really had any friends, just people who pretended to like me.

But with him, it was all different. I am different you know. I belong to a religion that modern day Christianity has condemned as evil. People never want to be associated with anyone who practices what I practice. However, before I could even tell him, he told me he has his own things too, so he does not care who says what.

This is the person who was there when no one was. Although he lived a parallel life, many lives, at least he was there. He was there for me. He was the father to my daughter, and he was my true friend.

Strangely enough, I never introduced him to my daughter.

The first time they met, I was not there. Apparently, he had left work early to go and do something. On the way, he got a lift with my mother. That day, as any other day, my mother would pick my daughter up from school. So that is how they met. I did not even know they had met. I remember, at the time, I had no interest in him. He would come and sit in my office for hours, but I just had no interest. Until this one day, he looked over my shoulder and saw my daughter's picture on the wall and complemented her for being "a nice kid". I did not even know they had met. When I asked about it, he just brushed it off as if he did not see that I was curious how and where they met. My daughter was only four years old then and this guy did not stay anywhere close to where we stayed so he could not have met her on the street. Even if he had met her, how did he know she was my daughter? I did not know and obviously I would not expect my four-year-old to remember everybody she had met.

He always reminds me that it was her first before me. She was the one who came into his life before me so their bond is different and no matter what, she would always be his first born.

This is a man who could have been with anyone, but yet decided to "stick around". Yes, there were a lot of "sticking" things in places I cannot mention and yes, he is by far the best thing anyone can ever have. I mean, there is good and there is good. He is the other good.

In all the mess we went through, in all the pain and humiliation we have endured, in all the promises made and broken, families supportive and against, conscience telling us this and that, one thing remains, I made a commitment to myself that I will love him unconditionally until death do us apart. To this day, that is what I am doing irrespective of where he is, what or who he is doing and how he feels about me. I will love him with all my heart. I will always pray for him more than I do for myself, I will always celebrate his achievements and mourn his loses. I will be happy for him when he is happy, be there for him when he is sad and that, nobody will ever take away from me. And yes, if he ever wants to, because he knows no one can touch it, he will always be welcome with open legs, I mean open arms.

He is my other self, and I am his unmarried wife.

Chapter 2

The First Encounter

It all started with that one visit. John, as I referred to him on more occasions than I can remember, had just received his employment offer as an intern. We called them trainees in our company. As most new employees would come through my office for one thing or another at the beginning of their employment, so did John. He was with a friend, so I thought at the time of which later on I found out that he was just a colleague who happened to be starting on the same day and the two happened to have met prior to that day. Apparently, they went to the same College.

The first time John laid eyes on me; I was sure he was developing an immediate interest. Him being shy and reserved, he did not say a word. I remember, I was wearing one of my tight black pants, a black top, a brownish throw jersey and as always, I was rocking one of my black ten-inch hills. My job allowed me to dress as I wished but always professional. The introduction was brief. "This is so and so; they are here for an internship. John is in a so and so department and James a so and so department. John and James, this is Aliana, she will give you everything you want. She is the madam of this department", said my boss, leaving them with me.

Throughout the whole process, the paperwork etc., I do not remember John saying a word. He just looked at me. Me being me, I decided to give him an even better look; I walked out of the office. If you know me, you would know that I can rock a catwalk. So, I did. Just for the fun of it.

Well, as one does not write their own destiny, instead of John talking, James did. He started small conversations about this and that. Things I cannot remember, but I do remember that he asked for my number. Honestly, I cannot remember whether I gave it to him or not, but he did get my number. Our numbers were on our email signatures, so anyone with email access would have any number they wanted. At the time John was just another trainee just like the hundreds I have seen coming in and out of my office in my long career with my then company. James was the one who showed interest. At the time, the two characters appeared to be very different, only to find out many years later that they are no different. Both have egos bigger than earth itself but the one is outspoken while the other is reserved.

Like any other day, I did not think much of that day. It was a normal day like any other day. I met new people as I always did in my job until that very same afternoon when my phone rang. Damn, it was James. He started with his small chats as he had done earlier that day, and boom, he asked me out. I am a nice person; I grew up around boys. I was more of a tomboyish girl than the lady people saw me as. So, an innocent outing with a guy would not hurt.

So, I agreed. Somewhere, somehow something happened; that date never materialized. During their stay at my workplace, both of them would come to my office for one thing or the other. Every time James did, he was on to one thing, a date. Every time John came, he was also on one thing, give me that stir. I could see he wanted to say a lot, but I guess he chose not to. Sometimes I would think he is just a wimp but other times I would think he was just not into people like me. He was an intern, and I was already a couple of years working. I spoke fluent English which he made it clear that he does not like.

He felt that people who speak English to their fellow countrymen are just coconuts.

He would make it a point to respond in his home language. Well, we are both came from similar language backgrounds, so I did understand.

One day, just before their tenure ended, John asked for my number. I gave it to him; I think he had already had it but just wanted to see if he was allowed to call.

I waited, I waited, and I waited. But he never called. Until one day, many months after they left. Actually, it was around two or three months. I got a phone call. "Hi, it's John, that guy who came there with the other guy and you showed no interest in him and only focused on the other guy". I was perplexed, why did this guy speak in such riddles. At least he had my number and at least he had called, so I decided to listen. He was brief. He is a straightforward person who does not really enjoy small chats. So, he was very brief.

"Well, I just wanted to see if the number still works. I am at another site for another internship. Sho, bye".

My then organization had a number of operations in different cities. He was in one of our south operations while my site operation was further east. The other site was a couple of hundreds of miles away to be exact.

I did not think much of that call. Between then and the time we finally met in person again, we had exchanged a few emails. It was mostly the "hi, how you doing?" sort of emails.

A year later, he returned to the operation I was based at. This time around he was in a different internship. I swear I never understood these internships. Some would take a month or two, others a couple of months and some would take up to three or four years. Most of them were chronological. So, from one internship, you would go to the next, etc. until you get your permanent employment placement. This time around he was a little different. He could hold a conversation with anyone and even if it was a topic you could tell he had no interest in.

He had friends, or should I say, close colleagues, because he always wanted me to understand that he does not have friends. I can therefore say he had close colleagues. Most of them were guys I had known for some time. Some were from my neighbourhood. Most had tried their luck with me, but me being me, it was all in vain, except for one who got way too close if I may say so myself. He was my boyfriend, so people used to say. It had not been long since those rumours came out, John started talking to me.

He would make it a point that if he sees this guy coming towards our building, he would also come and start small chats. John is very arrogant I must say. He is the "I don't give an f***" type of a person. Sometimes he would do something just for the sake of pissing you off and he enjoyed it. With all that commotion going on, people started taking sides. Some felt that John was too much of himself and he wanted everything for himself. Knowing John, "Everything" meant one thing, "everyone". This guy was not impressed at all. He felt disrespected. Besides, he had gone through some difficulties himself at work since at that time I was seeing someone. Someone in a very high position. So, he felt disrespected by John and everyone who was on John's side.

When John heard that I was seeing this other guy in a high position, it appeared as if John had received some boost. As he had put it many years later, he wanted to prove that it is not about what one has, but what one does with what they have. He was determined to throw his management team member under the bus. Strangely enough, he never mentioned anything about him when we spoke, but I could tell by some of his comments that all he wanted was to prove that he can have somebody who thinks they belong to a different class than him.

I was made to find out at a later stage that there was a bet amongst the guys that John would never get me.

I moved with a different class, and I had once told him that I do not date his kind, I only do other races. This guy was a manager with a very high position.

John was just a trainee. He had no car, he rented a small room in the slums, he did not speak much of any English, he came from a very poor background while I already had a job, came from a decent family, going out with someone in a high position and I was older than him. Technically, there was nothing common between John and I. We were that different.

Instead of this discouraging John, it actually seemed to fuel him up. Now that I write this, I must admit, at some point I felt that maybe John really loved me. But, apart from us talking about my daughter, there was nothing much in common. He had met my daughter, without my knowledge and that was when he started pushing his agenda. He always now and again claimed that it was for the better good of my daughter to consider his relationship proposal. I never understood what he meant but then sometimes it made sense. He was a "nobody" at the time, but he was a man determined to make something out for himself. He did not care about his class standard; he developed enough courage to even start the topic even after I had made it clear to him that I had no interest in him. To be honest, I was more not interested in what he was not who he was. I did not know much about him. He was and still is a very secretive person. So, no one ever truly understands him. It is like he lives in his own world.

He was determined not to fail.

Even after an incident whereby my then partner found out and tried to get him out of the company because people had told him that this John seems to be getting way too close to me. He never backed down.

It was exactly a year and two months when one Friday evening, as usual, he was in my office. I think he enjoyed walking me out to the parking lot.

It made him rub it in to those who thought I would not even entertain him. He was in my office. It was my colleague, him and I. My colleague said, in passing, "maybe you should just give him a chance" and she walked out. She was already rushing for her transport. He looked at me with those ever-curious eyes and said "well, she's right".

Somehow, I did not think much of it. It was a festive season. Everybody was in a festive mood. I wanted to get out. I had made arrangements with my partner to meet that evening in town. I was going to catch a taxi as usual and when I was done with whatever I was doing, he would come and pick me up. So, I looked at John and just said "yah maybe we should give it a try".

Since we had known each other for over two years, we had spent countless hours each day together, we sort of had for some time acted as a couple, so it was not a strange thing for me to agree to go with him. At that time, he stayed in town since he was still attending classes in town in the evenings and on weekends, so he said.

I could see the excitement in his eye. I am sure he called one of his friends to collect on their bet that "tonight is the night, I'm in".

I also did not think much of it. For me, at least I had a place to hang at while waiting for my partner.

For the first time that evening, I saw where he stayed. As soon as he had signed me in and we entered his apartment, he left, for a brief period. Like I said, I grew up around guys so I can say most times I know how they think. Although we had never spoken about it to date, I am pretty sure he left to get protection. I am sure he was sure that he was getting some that evening.

His room was a decent room. Had a bed, a television, a fridge, a study table and a chair. He had books everywhere. He enjoyed school; that much I knew.

For him, it was his only hope of getting out of poverty. To him, when it came to schoolwork, anything would stop. It was always school first, work second, then the rest.

As most women have experienced that first day you visit a guy. He would be shifting left and right. He would be trying to touch you but not know where to start. He would not be sure whether you even want to be touched or not.

For John, it was an even uphill battle than most guys

had experienced. John is a very proud man. If you know proud and egoistic men, you would know they despise failure and rejection. So, he was very careful about it. I think he was also still wondering if I meant what I said when I said maybe we should try and see what happens. He, as being that careful guy he is, asked if I meant it. As soon as I said yes, he tried to shift forward for a kiss. One kiss, things started heating up. I was definitely not going to allow him to go any further than the kiss.

I crunch my teach thinking, why can't this man just call. I had not told John that I was actually in town to meet my partner. I was only with him to kill time until my partner picked me up. As time went by and kisses got more and more serious and intense, things heating up a bit, feeling the heat in all the wrong places, "ring ring" my phone rang.

I do not remember the sequence of events but all I can recall is that I stood up, packed my bag, told him someone is waiting for me downstairs and walked out.

I proceeded with my plans for that evening. I never heard anything from John for the remainder of the festive season. The day was our last day at work for that year. We were only going to return the following year after the festive holidays. I never called and he also never called.

I now know that he actually went and checked who was picking me up, so I guess he was pissed that I was leaving him after leading him into thinking he was about to achieve his goal. I say that with confidence because it happened that many years later, he admitted that the main bet with his colleagues was that he can get me into bed. Unfortunately, or fortunately for me, in the process, he fell in love. That is the period when I said he was in love with me while I was not. It was the beginning of a crazy life for John and Aliana.

I went on with my plans as planned and I do not know what happened with John. I know that the following day he went back home for the holidays and probably was skimming about his next move.

It was only until the following year that I saw him. It sounds like a long time, but it was only about two weeks. After getting to know him better as time went by, I am sure he called somebody to take my place that evening. I actually believed that is what he had done. He had a reputation when it comes to women. At some point in time, he said that to him, that was the turning point. That is the day he realized that maybe these feelings were for real. He was so shuttered that he could not even think about calling anyone and he could not be with anyone during that festive season.

He was in love. He hated what I was. He hated everything about my life. He hated all my companions. He even hated the guy he thought I was going out with in my neighbourhood. He sure despised my partner, thinking that he was using his status to get what he wants. At the time John did not know that this man had been on my side during one of my most difficult times. I even called him "milky" because he once tried to tap my boobs forgetting that they had milk. So, the milk splashed all over him. At the time, I must admit, I had no interest in John.

I was with this man. He loved me, so I thought. But later on in life I would realize that I was just his possession. He was a very strange man. He was a man who had been through a very difficult relation with his then wife who was then an ex-wife when I met him. He had caught her red-handed with someone else in bed. It had shattered him. I am sure it is an experience he would never want to talk about. I can talk about it because I heard it from John many years later.

Apparently during John's first arrival for the very first internship, he was transported to the motel by this guy. They got a bit close. So, you can imagine how he felt when he realized that John was venturing into what he considered his territory. Apparently, as I would hear it later on in life, he spoke a lot about me to John and James. A normal thing to do, looking at his age, would have been to ask him if he was married. Well, so did John and James. I am sure it was James though because at that time John was still a very reserved person. When they asked him about his wife, fortunately he had healed. Apparently, he told them everything. He told them what his wife had done to him was unforgivable. To him, women were some creatures that needed to be controlled because if you do not, you will find yourself in a psychiatric hospital due to stress. At that time, he was talking to these two interns who were there for a brief period, and they would probably never meet again. He did not anticipate that someday they may actually even meet his current possession. That was me by the way. The major breakup of him and his wife apparently happened at the very same motel John was staying at. So being curious as always, he asked the personnel working at the motel about it and everybody knows the stuff, they just sang. They told him how the relationship was and how it ended. Like I said, they just sang.

At the time, both men knew each other's positions at work. My partner was determined that John does not get anywhere closer to what he was to me.

He knew that nothing would ever happen at work, so he did not care much but he wanted to make sure that John never gets a chance to see me outside work. I think his sixth sense told him that John would not back down, and he was afraid that I may even fall for John. Until today, I still believe that he had seen us getting into the same taxi at work that afternoon because when he came by to pick me up, he was not in a very jolly mood. He had always been a moody, controlling person but he was good to me at most times. I felt protected around him. I was also a broken soul at the time. I had just had a child under very complicated and sensitive circumstances, so I did not know any better. He was the better. He was the person. John was just a guy who just came by and is trying his luck.

That evening, things did not go too well for me. I cannot remember much, or should I say, I do not want to remember much about it. But I think it was the beginning of the end for my relationship with that guy.

There was now John. As much as he hated everything I represented, what I was, what I did, what life I lived, he fell in love with the person. He fell in love with Aliana as a person. Today it reminds me of his philosophy that "what you are, comes and goes, it's contextual, it is guided by the environment you are in, but who you are is what always matter". Maybe he saw the person in me. He saw some good in me. He saw hope. He saw a person rather than a possession. He saw a mother because he sure loved my daughter. That day, John saw something.

That something is the thing that has made me make a commitment to love him eternally, with all his flaws, love the "who" in him not the "what" around him. Yes, there were a lot of things to like around him but to me; it started not to matter anymore.

This guy had chosen the person in me, so I felt justified to choose the person in him. This guy had treated me like a human being, like I matter, like my life matters. He was a fresh breathe of air. I could be whole with him. I did not have to pretend to be something I was not. Most importantly, I was not scared.

I am and will always be his Unmarried Wife.

Chapter 3

The New Chapter

The new season commenced. Everyone was back at work. John was back, I was back, and everyone was back. I did not know how John would look at be after that stunt I had pulled that other day. I was beginning to think that maybe he would not even want to talk to me. I was preparing myself for being looked at as a bad person. What was the worst that could happen? Already a lot of people believed that I liked men any way. John himself believed that too. So, what was the worst that could happen if he never talks to me again?

I had a life before him, and I will have one after him. He was not the only person who saw something in me. Whatever that was, it was something some other people also wanted. I was certain there were a lot of men who wanted me out there. I was sure a lot of men would die to have me. So, it was fine, I would be fine, everything would be fine, that's what I told myself. John would get over it. He would move on with his life. People do that right?. People move on with their lives if something does not work out. It is a normal thing to do. Normal people do that all the time. So, John would be fine. He would move on.

I was sure he had already moved on since he never called for the entire holiday period.

But then, I did not count on one thing; John was not normal. John was, is and will always be different. He does things his own way. It is always about his way or no way. If he says something; that is the only truthful thing to him at that point in time irrespective of what the evidence may be showing. In short, John does not care what others think or say.

It was a busy day. The happy New Year, the

compliments for the season were going on around the office. People were going around wishing others a prosperous year and all those things. John did not. He just came back to work, he said. He said that irrespective of how many wishes people wish for you, the year would just turn out exactly how it would have turned out even if no one had wished you a prosperous new year.

Low and behold, "he was there", in my office. I almost said that out loud. That would have been an embarrassing moment for me. At the time, I was not really comfortable with the decision I had made the previous year. I was not even sure if I had any feelings for him. So, it would have been very awkward to get excited just by seeing him in my office. He would have thought that maybe I was trying to brush away what had happened. For I had learnt that people like him do not forget, they are not scared to speak their mind out. I knew John would talk if he wanted to. He would ask whatever question he wanted to ask. What I would not do was to start the topic that would just be plain awkward.

But he was there. Standing right in front of me in my office. I still believe that I heard him calling me the "b" word. I do not know whether it was in my head, or it actually happened. I do not think he could say something like that. He was a nice guy after all. But I do think that he did, and he meant for me to hear it, yet he was not loud enough to appear as if it is directed to me. He just mumbled it.

He did not mention anything about the incident. He was there just to see if I was ok, and I said I was but the picture of his face when I left that day was still in my memory. I had hurt him and hurt him dearly. There is no worst thing you can do to a man that is more hurtful than hurting his ego. That was what I had done.

Maybe it was not about what I would think of him but about what he would think my partner thinks of him. He hated being dis-respected. He hated it with a passion.

We started talking about whatever it was. When we finished, he walked out acting as if nothing had happened. I was a bit concerned but happy at the same time. "So, he doesn't hate me", Good, he can keep whatever he is feeling to himself. I would just go with the flow. I was, after all, his girlfriend by then. I had agreed to be his girlfriend. I had to make a decision. I had to choose between the two. Do I remain a possession or do I go with someone who appears to be genuine? I had to make that choice. It was either John or my partner, but it could not be both. No, no ways. These two would murder each other if they ever found out. They both had strong characters.

As days and months went by, my relationship with John grew stronger. I was falling in love also. I was in love. I was in love for the first time in many years. I was in love with someone who thinks I was the best thing that has ever happened to him in this world. I was in love with someone who spoke about my daughter more than about my sexy body. Well, even if I have to admit it myself, I do have a sexy body. I look after my body. That is one of the very few things I like about myself. Apart from that, I'm a bit of a mess.

I was in a catch 22 situation. I loved this guy. I loved John but John is a good guy. A guy focused on his studies, work and making a living. He had future plans. It was like his life was a project. Everything had to fall in place at the right time. He was one person whom failure was his biggest enemy. Failure and poverty were and are still his biggest fears in life. He was there, loving someone like me. I was a mess. I was a mess as a person both emotionally and spiritually.

Would he ever really accept me for who I am? I wondered. At the time all that mattered was that I was happy, and he appeared happy too. The rest, I told myself, only time would tell, and it sure did.

By this time my family already knew him. Strangely

enough, my mother actually liked him. They had their own relationship. Sometimes my mother would ask him to come fix things at home if they were broken. So, I can say they were fine with each other.

My family is a very close family. We lived together with my sister, brother, mother and my daughter.

My father had passed on many years prior. He too was a good man. Everyone has their flaws, but he was a good man. I came from a family of mixed religions. This may not make sense why I am mentioning it now, but it is one of the cornerstones of my whole life. My whole life especially from the time I met John. My extended family too was a family of mixed religions. Sometimes some religious people do not want to accept the existence of another religions. So, I was the outcast in my immediate family. We were close but there were things I knew they would never understand or accept. There were things that I did not think any man would embrace and understand. I was different. I am different. My religion is but the pillar of my strength and my weakness. Now I have grown to embrace it too. Back in the days, when I was younger, I used to be sort of ashamed of it. I was technically ashamed of myself. I would hide it from the public. Most people around me did not know about it. It was better that way. Society likes to judge people based on their religion. I was not about to allow myself to go through all that explanation to everyone. I kept it to myself and obviously a few people that knew about it.

Strangely enough, John knew about it too. He asked once, in passing and I pretended as if I did not hear him.

He was not religious at all, but he portrayed a particular religion which was against who I was. It did not seem to bother him much. He would notice small things that I thought an outsider would not notice. For instance, as early as we were in our relationship, he understood that there were things that cannot just happen.

He did not seem to have a problem with it. He even

noticed that my relationship with my mother was not normal. We were close, yes, but there were some limitations. John seemed to suggest that the reason was because of my religion. After asking many questions one day, he just concluded that the main reason my mother and I were not close was because she was the one who should have taken the spirits I have. She was the one who should be following the religion I am in. But because she delayed it and denied its existence, it had to be me. I am the first born after all. He even once said that the biggest problem is that when I suffer, my mother actually feels even worse than me because deep down, she knew why I was suffering.

I was a loner when it comes to religion. I had cut out most of the people I thought were friends. I could no longer go out. I was either at home, at work or with John. John was a loner too. The difference is that, for him, it was easy, he enjoyed it, and he grew up like that, so he enjoyed being a loner. He would emphasise on numerous occasions that he is not lonely, he is just alone, or a loner and he was fine with that.

When I got comfortable with talking about it, I told him as much as I could about my past life. I was as honest as I could. I wanted him to be certain that he knows what he is getting himself in for. However, I misrepresented one small detail about something that would later comeback to affect everything about our relationship. At the time, I thought it was the right thing to do.

I could not lose them or open any possible gap between him and my daughter. It was just something I could not do.

They were close. They were getting even closer. My daughter was growing up. She had a father now. All was well. She even called him daddy. Most women know how much of a struggle it is to introduce someone to your child. For me, I was fortunate. They met on their own. I remember even the day she first called him daddy. He was visiting as he usually did. One thing though, he never entered the house. He would just stay on the street in front of my house, and we would go to him.

This one day, my daughter looked at him and out of the blue she just asked him if it was ok to call him daddy and he said yes. That was it. From that day onwards she called him daddy. Until this day, I cannot remember a day she called him by name even when she talks to someone else. When they walk at a mall, she would just introduce herself as his daughter. He is her father and will always be. Their relation, as now she is a teenager, is so deep that she would even want his input about what to do in the head, what hairstyle to do. If it was up to her, she would have removed her dreadlocks long ago, but daddy said "no". As of this moment, she still has her dreadlocks.

Our relationship was not what most people would dream of. There were a lot of people around us who did not want to see it succeeding. To make things worse, we worked together. He would make it a point that he rubs it off to them and that would push them even harder to start spreading rumours.

Because they could see and they knew what he stood for, most of the rumours were about me. In their eyes, I was not worthy of such a good guy. But to some, he was also not worthy of me. They thought I deserved better. John was not a friendly person, but he had a way around women. Even as for the women, some women, knowing very well that I am there, would still want to go out with him. My biggest concern was that I knew the type of a person he was. He could not be just a friend.

He could not hold small talks or go out for movies or something. So, if there were any rumours about any girl, I was certain he was sleeping with her. Some, I knew were rumours but some I know for a fact they were real.

Somehow, some would say love is blind, instead of fighting him, I would fight them. Not physically of course, but I would rub it on them that they are just a tap and go material, they are not worthy of his commitment, they would never replace what we had. Well, I was right. None of them did. I do not even believe that there was one that would stay longer than one or two meetings with him. He was not that type. People would not understand him like that. Sometimes he just wanted his space. He would just go mute for no reason, and he would justify it with "if I have nothing to say, why do I need to talk?". That was it. I understood him like that. He was very short-tempered too. So, because he was not violent, if anything upset him, he would just keep quiet. Funny enough, many years later in our relationship, I remember he would drive from town to pick me up and we would not say a word to each other. We would go do what we wanted to do, and he would drop me back home without saying a word.

That was John, he was one strange character. So, I knew no one would tolerate that. For me, I loved him like that. He kept me sane. He kept me calm. He actually gave me another reason to progress in life. My daughter was always one, now there was him. He was God sent.

Chapter 4

The Ins and Outs

It was then a norm; we would meet a couple of days a week. All our meetings were mostly about one thing. He did not talk much so there was nothing to talk about. He was busy with his career, and I was busy with, well, nothing that I can remember. I know he hated that. He used to say that it was pity that kids from good middle schools turn out to attend private colleges or do unnecessary courses. To him, most private colleges' courses were just for people who want to remain at an entry level. Partially he was correct. Most of the courses we did were very basic. The industry is made up of people who went to traditional public universities, so their view of the private colleges is not good. Sometimes I feel like they are just spiting us for going to good schools. The truth though, in this country, these private colleges do not help much if one does traditional mainstream courses. They would have to compete with people from traditional universities. Probably the entire management team would be from the traditional universities. So, it never works out too well for private college graduates.

For him, school was everything. It was his comfort zone. It was where he felt at home. For as long as I have known him, he has always been studying something or working on some project.

By project, I do not mean, me, I mean academic or work-related project. I was a different project. I was a project that he used to prove something to himself. I am not certain what exactly but one of the things was that he wanted to prove to himself that he is not as bad as people think he is. He can change a person. He can give a person a reason to want to live to see another day. Talking about living, strangely enough, it did not matter much to him.

He always said that if he were to ever die at any point

in time, He would be glad. He had achieved things most people around him never thought he could. First it was people who knew his background. It was very hard to come from the countryside and make something worthy for your life. Secondly, his character or personality did not fit anywhere. Even at work, he had very few people on his side. His attitude was that he was hired to do a job and as long as he does it well, he sees no reason to want to fit in. He never cared who would listen to him or take his side. He would just say what he wanted to say and that was it. If anyone did not agree, he would just say "ok". To him though, whatever he had said remained. He was like that. He is like that. He can make what appears to be the dumbest decision and yet feel nothing. He would say, "it's my decision not yours, so it shouldn't bother you. If you have any inputs, you are welcome to raise them, but it doesn't mean I will support them. This is what I say, and this is what it would be".

He was like that even in his personal life. Sometimes he would say something that did not make any sense at all to me but would never want to explain it.

He used to say, "why explain a statement, if a person doesn't get it, it means it doesn't matter to them". He hated repeating himself. Because he spoke so softly, sometimes even softer just to spite the person he was talking to, you had to concentrate when you talk to him. He would say that if you did not hear, it means you were not meant to hear it. So, its fine, life goes on. This attitude is not an attitude that takes anyone anywhere in life. He would say that "where I come from, it is dog eat dog environment, and we don't have time to over explain or beg". When we were having a conversation, I would have to listen attentively so that I could even pick up his cold humours.

One thing I hated the most was that the moment you ask him to repeat himself, no matter in what mood he was in, he would just shut off. Shut off as in, completely shut off. Now you would not know if you had said anything to offend him or what. Once that happens, you could kiss that day goodbye because it would take him forever to comeback to a good mood.

He would say that it takes him less than a second for his mood to go from 100 to 0 but it would take forever for it to move from 0 to even 50. He was or is a very moody person. He says he is not moody; he just does not have energy to entertain nonsense sometimes. Nonsense in his context is anything that does not make sense to him or that he deems irrelevant.

My technically-forced attentive listening was not easy. I am a bubbly person. I sure can talk. And I can talk a lot. But this time, I had to learn to keep quiet and listen. I had to learn to pay attention to small details. He would say something while meaning another. Months or weeks later when something happens, he would say "but I told you".

To him, what he meant was what meant. If you did not get it, it was your problem. So, I had to learn to listen more and talk less. At the time, it was just something I was doing to avoid upsetting him but later on, I realized that it was the best thing that has ever happened to me. I started learning to pay attention to small things, small details. It helped me more than it helped him. He always said, "It's for your own good". I never understood then but now I do. It helped me even pay attention to small details about myself. The people around me started to mean something totally different. I realized that I can be me. I can be myself. I can be the person I want to be from deep within not this character I portray so as to fit in. It built some confidence. I was now more confident about myself than I've ever been before.

I started focusing on important things. I did not have many friends anymore. It was my daughter first, him, myself, my family and I even started knowing his family. That was all that mattered to me. I did not care what people say or think about me. As long as I was happy, it did not matter.

It was not an overnight thing. It was not like I just woke up and started acting differently. It took some time.

It took some learning and mostly some unlearning of a lot of habits. I was a friendly, outgoing person. I had people I called friends. I was on the telephone literally all day and all night long amongst other things. He hated that.

After some time, when I was starting to focus on detail, to pay attention to small details, I started seeing patterns I had not noticed. Most of my so-called friends were male. Most of the time I spent on the telephone was with them. They would come to my house more often than I could count. It did not bother me though because they were just friends, and my family also knew them as friends. It felt like a normal thing to do. However, the more time I spent with John, the more I started noticing that these co-called friends were not real friends. Almost all of them had hidden agendas. They had ulterior motives. I started recalling all the events spent with them. Literally, all have had joked about wanting to go out with me at one stage or the other. It would be something that would come up and just be brushed off as friends being friends.

Friends are meant to joke around and say whatever they want to say to each other. Because to me, they were just friends, it was something that did not bother me that much, until now, until the very moment when I started paying attention. It became clear to me that what they actually wanted was to sleep with me someday. They were hoping I would pay attention to them when they start their nonsense someday and I would agree. I was like a pet chicken. To them, it was like having a chicken as a pet. You can pamper it for as long as you want but come thanksgiving night, you will eat it hot that day. You would turn it inside out; you would stick things in it that only you know where they have been. In short, having a chicken as a pet is just a waiting game.

Most of these guys liked to take me out. I thought it

was all innocent then, but later, I noticed that it was never about that. Not meaning to boast about my character, but I was an "I wish I could have a girlfriend like you type".

I would fit in with any friend they introduced me to. I would smile and go with the flow when they claim that I was their girlfriend. I dressed well, maybe too well for my liking now. I was seductive. I just had that look. So, it was convenient for them to keep me around. It gave them something to boast about while secretly praying that someday they would do me.

If there was one thing I was ever scared of, was to undress in front of a stranger. A stranger to me is anyone other than my family. So, it was actually never going to happen anyway. But you would never know. What if one day they drugged me, what if they kidnapped me or something? Who knows where I could have ended up? But thanks to John, all these small things started to make sense. They started to make me see things for what they are. So, I started cutting them off one by one. They were not very impressed. Most of them obviously blamed John. They felt that he was over-controlling. The funny part was that it was never him. He was never the type to want to know what is happening. He would say, "Your phone is your phone, and my phone is my phone, just tell your friends though not to call when I am around, and my phone will never ring when you are around as well". He was never the controlling type. However, for him, it was always "my way or the highway".

He would not enforce anything but would not hesitate to tell you when he does not like something. He would not even be telling you how he would like it; just that he does not like it. "It's your life after all", he would say.

Although he hardly ever mentioned it directly, he hated my job. He felt that I was too comfortable with nothing. I went to a good school, I messed it up by going to a private college, now I had a job that would never take me anywhere. It was a job that had very little prospects of promotion to high levels. So, to him, I was going to remain at an entry level of the working class. He always said he wanted someone who could afford themselves. As much as he is a man, he believed that a woman in his life needs to be able to afford themselves. In that case, they can grow together. If the women cannot afford themselves, it would mean that he would be working backwards because as things get more and more expensive, it means he would have to spend more and more on that woman instead of them building up something. It never made sense then, but it does not.

He never said it outright, but he wanted me to get a new job, a better job, a job that he can be proud of and a job that our daughter could be proud of. Because he knew how people's careers are a sensitive topic to them, he would not put it directly, but he would, on numerous occasions, mention that he would never stay in the same level for more than five years until he gets to a level he can retire at. In simplicity, he was just telling me that he thinks I had stayed for too long at my then position.

I had been in it for over five years and there were no automatic prospects of growth. For instance, one can stay at the same level for many years if they are still training because that has a direct prospect of promotion. If you are in a permanent position, you will stay there until you start looking for something different.

I had to do something about it. I had to move. I had to look for a course that would allow me to move, to grow. This was not going to be easy. I had not been studying for some time and the thought of sleepless nights with schoolbooks sent shivers down my spine. This man was different. He was just not enjoying the ride, but he wanted to make sure that I do become a better person.

During the later years of our relationship, I was frequenting his place more than often. We would do whatever we did, and he could actually leave me lying there and start with his books. I was definitely not going to replace his love for school. He would rather have me upset with him than miss an already planned hour to study. Fortunately, there was nothing to be upset about. When we did what we did, he would leave me so exhausted that I would actually fall asleep for some time. By the time I woke up, instead of maybe feeling that he is not paying enough attention to me and focusing on his books, it would be time for him to take a break too. Then we would again do whatever we wanted to, and I would be exhausted. He would proceed with his books. By the time I was well again, it would be time for me to go home and he knew that as that was also his time to take a break. It was a normal setup.

I am sure though, although he would never admit, that after he had dropped me off at home, he would not go back to his books, he would also sleep. That one is for sure. If you are an adult and doing adult stuff, you would understand what I mean. I was, if I say so myself, not at all that bad. I was actually very good. He said so himself. So, I know. Until today, I always know that he brought out the best in me, that is why I over performed.

Before your mind loses the moral of this story, he did bring out the best in me. In all aspects of my life. I was a better person. I was surrounded by fewer people who mattered.

I was no longer that girl who lived for the fun of it. I had a future. I had a future with someone who brought out the best in me.

It was never that glossy though, we had our moments. We fought, not physically; he was never physical at all. He took out his frustrations in all the right places through all the right positions. Our fights were mostly about one thing. It was about one suspecting the other was cheating. He never wanted to call it cheating. To him, cheating is when you love more than one person; it has nothing to do with how many people you are sleeping with. It was either there were rumours that I was sleeping with someone or that he was sleeping with someone.

To date, I can happily say that there was never a point in time when he found any proof. But I cannot say the same with him. Some of these girls used to want to rub it in on me so I can say that most of the rumours about him were true. He would sleep around sometimes.

He would deny it though every time I confronted him. It hurt me dearly. I used to ask myself why because I believed that I was exactly what he wanted. I never questioned him on most occasions, I understood his moods. I was almost perfect where it mattered the most for him, where he took out his frustrations and I was certain there are things he could never do with these other girls. He could not even hold a conversation with them. I felt that maybe I was not good enough for him, I was not successful enough or educated enough. But these girls were even worse than me. That was what gave me comfort. I knew that it would never amount to anything but booty calls with them. If he did not want to be seen with them in public, what makes them think he would choose them over me. He would even deny them in front of their faces. Now why would he deny them? It could only be because he never cared whether they see him again or not.

Some of them thought it was fun. They thought it was a game. A game to fool me. He would deny them in front of my face and they would play along, yet I would still hear that they went to see him. Some were so silly that they did not mind knowing that there is someone else rumoured to be with him as long as it was not me, they were fine.

It was not an easy relationship. He was not as perfect as I paint him out to be to people. But I made a commitment to myself. His shortfalls are his alone. I may know about them, but I could never allow anyone to know and use them against him. He was still my king.

All I had to do was to play my part. Let him be, allow him to make his own mistakes. Let him learn from them and I was certain that someday it would stop. I was never all that perfect myself too. So why would I expect him to be perfect. No, I could not. I loved him the way he was. He used to brush the arguments off by calling them "3rd Degree". When I started with them, he would just say "are you here for 3rd Degree or for me?". Now at that moment, I knew he was not interested in talking about it.

I knew if I proceeded with the topic, he would just tell me to leave or he would leave. He was so strange that he could leave anytime, even just when we were about to do the hanky-panky deeds. He was that type of a guy.

As stupid as it may sound, that part of it gave me comfort. I knew that he probably takes these girls to his place and never actually sleep with them because they either had a bra or a panty he did not like, or they said something he did not like. Worse, normal people like food. For him, once you talk about food, you are out. He would switch off completely. Once he switches off, he cannot do anything. At least I knew that much about him.

Chapter 5

The Perceived Future

The perfect future was on the cards. We were madly in love. We had decided to disregard what outside people were saying. We were going to be the couple of the century. So, we thought. Should I say, so I thought. We had support everywhere. Support from no one. Not even our families. I am not certain about him, but my family was always skeptical about him. My mother had a problem with all the rumours about him and these other girls. Even one of my quietest brothers was not taking too kindly to him. They thought that he was embarrassing me. He was mocking and making fun of my love for him. They did not understand why I was with someone who disrespected me this way, according to them.

On his side, I would never know whether his family was in support or not, but at least they played along. He was the type his family never questioned. He would tell them that everybody should live their lives and allow others to do the same. He would say that if he needed any input, he would ask for it. Apart from that, people should just let him be. It was not helpful that his family was not one of the socially normal families too. So, he used this notion to avoid any interference in his private life. His mother had separated from his father when he was a kid.

His father had been married three or four times after that. He had close to 20 kids all over and was supporting only about 3 or four of them, the rest were taken care of by their mothers. John himself was never supported by his father. He grew up with a single mother who did odd jobs just to get by.

None of his Father's side and Mother's side family had normal family setup either according to societal norms. Either there were single parents, unhappy marriages, unsupportive fathers, etc. so to him, no one in his entire family had any right to tell him how to handle relationships.

He would deal with it his own way. He had convinced himself that he knew what he was doing. He had been through a lot in life but yet has come out ok. He now had a University Degree, he had a good job, he was able to support himself and help his mother out. He was ok. He believed that he knew how to take care of himself. He was then in no mood to have anyone comment about our relationship. It was an either you accept it, or you just keep quiet about it. I could say he was a little bit rebellious. Well, maybe not a little, but his rebelliousness was well calculated. You could never see it when it came to serious things. To him, serious meant school and work. In society, he deemed everything subjective. He would say that no one in this world has the best interest of any other person but themselves. That is why he would choose what and who to listen to as and when he feels like it. That was his approach too in our relationship.

He would use this attitude even during all our arguments.

He would say that people say whatever they want to say. He would also argue that there is no point in whether denying or acknowledging any allegations. He would say that it did not matter what the response was because he would give whatever response he wanted. Whether the response was truthful or not, it was irrelevant. It was even least relevant because it would not matter what he had said, what would matter was what I believed. It therefore did not matter whether he says anything or not because I would still believe whatever I wanted to believe.

He would try and justify it by a long confusing statement until I give up.

He would say, "You know, I do not see any reason for you asking me all these questions. These are rumours you heard from somewhere. They were spread by someone. You do not even know who started them. Even if you did, you don't know why they did. Was it because the rumours are true or not, is it because they want you to hear them and hurt you, is it because they care so much about you that they are trying to protect you? you will never know. You heard the rumours and you concluded. If you hadn't concluded, you would not be asking me this. So, whatever I say is irrelevant because you already have concluded. Even if I do say anything, it might be true or not and you would never really know whether it was true or not. The way I look at it, there are rumours going around, you heard them, you mentioned to me that you know about them, and that should be it. We should just move on with life. If I were to entertain every rumour I hear about you, we would be on permanent 3rd Degree sessions".

To some extent he was right. I have learnt that sometimes it does not matter what a person says, what matters is what you hear. A person would say whatever they want to say based on the circumstances they are faced with. Truthfulness is subjective. People say the truth never changes and the truth will set you free. I am not sure, "set you free" from what exactly. The truth can change your life forever. It can change it drastically negatively. Take a simple example, after, say 65 years of believing that your father passed on when you were 2 years old, how would the truth of finding out that he actually left you because he never believed you were his biological child, how would that truth make you feel. At that age, you would probably collapse and die of a heart attack. In essence, the truth is just that, it has no power over anything. It is what it is and can result in as much as what lies can result to.

As time went by, I realized that there was some truth in his analysis of life. He would say that in most cases, it is never about right or wrong, it is about winning or losing, and people would do anything to win even if it means lying.

Looking at some of the lies I have told him, some of them which I have yet to even try and correct, I think I understand what he meant. I also had lied to him a number of occasions. He would be upset for some time and eventually stop worrying about it. He sure does not forget, and he would remember every single word in a conversation he held many years ago.

I can then say, his family had no choice but accept it as is. It was his relationship after all, not theirs.

On my side, my family also somehow gave up. Although they were not happy, they accepted that it was a decision I should make on my own.

We were in the world of our own. We were going to disappear to somewhere where no one knows us, we would live a live that we decide for ourselves, we would not take comfort to anyone who thinks normality is what society describes it as but what we deem normal. We were content with being abnormally-normal. That was our normal.

We had started some sort of a cult. It was a cult of two. We would hate each other so much that the only way of punishment was super rough bedroom sessions. It was like we were high on something. Somehow every time there was an issue to resolve, this would be the only way to do it. After that session, you would never hear a word about it. Life would move as if nothing had happened. Besides, he was never interested in discussing relationship things anyway. He would say that relationships are not his things. His life is like this, and a person just need to understand. If they do not, well, hard luck.

There were talks of marriages, kids, etc. but I must admit, that was mostly from my side. He never entertained such. He would just change a topic when it came up in a conversation. He used to say these little bambinos are just a headache. He never wanted his own biological kids.

His biggest fear was that if it were to be a girl, what if she meets and falls in love with someone like him, if he was a boy, what if he turns out just like him. It was something he could never contemplate. He knew that he was not a socially acceptable character, but he could never change it because it was a character he adopted for survival.

It protected his feelings; it gave him something to be proud of. People would try getting to understand him, but the least people did, the more exciting it was for him. Somehow, I feel like he enjoyed being disliked.

I was happy too. I was in love. We were in our own world. Things were looking up. My daughter was doing well in school, my mother had gotten around to accepting him the way he was, my family was starting to warm up to him too. Things were fine. My family would even complain why he never came into the house. I would have to bring him food to his car parked outside the gate. No matter what, he would not get into the house. Even if he did, it would be for a few minutes, and you would see that he was not comfortable. Up to date, I think I can count the number of times he had been inside my house. I am sure it is less than ten and there were seriously valid reasons for it, except that one day. That day, well, we were just being who we know best. Sometimes one cannot control the animal in them.

And then, my other life started acting up. The problem with my religion was that the more you try to avoid it, the more problem it would cause for you. First, it was my daughter. She started getting sick. Every time she got sick, I felt that it had something to do with me. Then it was me. I started getting sick, very sick. This was always a problem between my mother and I. She knew that once it starts, I would have to perform certain rituals she did not accept. Fortunately, we still had a home; my grandmother's house was far away from where we were staying. I would then go to my grandmother's house to do whatever I had to do. The sickness never stopped. It just got worse and worse. I had to do something. Whatever I had to do would affect everything around me. My family would be affected, my daughter would be affected, and this perfect world of John and I would definitely be affected. Although I knew John did not have a problem with my religion, I did not picture him accepting this level of rituals. This would mean that I could not see him for months after months and I would not be able to do certain things for months, even years, depending on how it went.

I had to make a choice. Well, I did not have much of a choice. He was one of the reasons why I was getting sick. I did not want to explain anything to him. He understood. I just had to tell him how long it would take.

Now, this may be something that may seem irrelevant to some people but in my community, a very few people accepted my religion. It was even worse for him because it was like a taboo for a guy to go out with someone like me, unless that guy also subscribes to the same religion.

At first, it was fine because only close people knew about it. It was something that the general public could not automatically tell. But this time around, I had to start dressing up in a particular way which would show everyone what I am. Should I say, who I am?

At work, people would start talking, his family would start talking, even worse, and he would also have a problem because he knew his grandmother would never accept anyone who belongs to this religion. He had a very close but distant relationship with his grandmother. He believed that he was what he was because of her. He could never disappoint her. Not even without here knowing. It was a self-conscious thing for him. So, this was going to be tough. For everyone around me, it was sure the beginning of the end. The world as I knew it was ending. I could never do normal work again, I could never dress up as I wished or go wherever I wanted, do whatever I wanted, and I had to subscribe to my religion. Some of my family members were sure that it was the end between John and

I. People at work were also happy that eventually we would break up. This was it; it was the beginning of the end. It was the end of our little fairy tale. I was going to my religion initiation, he was carrying on with his life, he would find someone else, do all the things we used to do which I could no longer do, and he would eventually forget about me.

To my surprise, he stuck by. He would actually laugh it off as if it was no big deal. It was a big deal. A really big one. But he would just laugh it off.

At some point, he would even wake up at night to go pick me up and take me to where I was supposed to go. Until now, I never understood why he did it because it was never because of love. He never believed in love the way we know love as. He would say "love is not for everyone; it is for those who believe in it". He would never explain though whether he believed in it or not. He used to say love is a feeling like any other feeling. It comes and goes as and when it feels like it just like happiness, sadness, hunger, anger, excitement, tiredness, etc. They are just feelings, and no feeling is eternal. It all ends at some point and sometimes come back.

So, it could never have been for love. Maybe he felt sorry for me, maybe he felt sorry for my daughter; that is one thing I would never know. All I know is that he was there when I needed someone the most. He took a lot of ridicule from people especially at work, but he stayed by. He waited for me to complete whatever I was doing.

The one thing I always appreciated about him was that although he grew up in a particular religion, he considered himself as a neutralist. His definition of a neutralist was someone who does not belong to any religion but accepts and acknowledges all other religions. He was a neutralist but avoided by all means to be part of any religious gathering. At the end of my initiation, for a person who had supported me so much, it would have been a normal thing to attend the ceremony. But no, he did not. He had no excuse for it but just did not attend. I was hurt but I understood.

After all, he had always said that he is happy for whichever religion a person belongs to, but they should never try to sell their religion to him. He has his own relationship with the Creator, and no one will convince him otherwise.

This was a man who had endured a lot of hurtful statements and rumours regarding what actually goes on during initiations. He had all the right reasons to walk away. I would have been hurt but I would have understood. Instead, he remained. He even started fantasying about stupid things in relation to what I now was. We would laugh at it as if it was a normal thing. He remained. He never changed a bit. This is the man I had made a commitment to myself to love him eternally. And I was there, I loved him. I was committed to him, even more so then than before. He was the only person who could touch me. I was his forever, and I was not about to go through all the headache of trying to be normally normal again. I was content with being abnormally normal. He was content with it too.

I sometimes think he actually enjoyed it more than I had anticipated. He knew he was safe. I could never leave anymore. If I did, there would be a lot of things I would have had to do. So, he was safe. We were going to stick together through thick and thin. My thin had just passed. His thin was yet to come. I did not know what it would look like. I did not know how easy or difficult it would be, but I would also stick with him through thick and thin. I was going to be there, I am there, I will always be there. I am his unmarried wife after all.

Every time I think about it, I always remember that one message I sent him when I thought I was losing him. It was short and straight to the point, and I am sure he understood how I felt. It read: "I will always be proud of the man I watched grow up in front of my eyes. I will always be proud of the Father of my kids. I will always be proud of the boy that loved this girl and grew her up to be a woman. I will always be proud of the son whom that my mother prides herself of. I will always be proud of the man you have become despite everything, and you will always be my husband, the father of my kids, luv luv, luv bug". By the way, he hated being called "Luv bug". He said it did not matter what it implied, the point is, and he is not a bug. "Humans cannot be called bugs". Well, he liked to correct everything. I guess that why I loved him. He perfected me. That must have been hard. I was never an easy person to deal with. My memories of him in me are very vivid. He taught me a lot. I know he did not think he did, but he did. He was the man I met at work many years ago. He was the man I thought was full of himself but as time went on, I fell in love with him despite his full of himself appearance and when I did, I knew very well that he was indeed full of himself, but I loved him even more.

Chapter 6

The Imperfect Life

Sometimes life just throws you curveballs. John was full of himself. He also thought I was full of myself. But now I know that if we were both not full of ourselves, we would not have lasted a day.

I grew older, wiser and stronger due to all the heartaches he had put me through. I knew he was skeptical about our age gap, however, he always brushed it off. I was, at some point also skeptical about the age gab, but by then, it mattered not. If it were to matter, it would have mattered when we first met. I saw us as equals then. Even more so, he was much more matured than his age, so the age issue never really became a point to be concerned about.

We had been together for almost a decade then. You can imagine how much people grow in a decade. We have weathered all the storms that you can think off. We were still standing still. I was still standing still. I had become more resilient than I could ever imagine. He had taught me well. He had shaped me into someone I never even contemplated in my past life. I then had a new job. I had studied further and managed to secure myself a better job at the same organization. My daughter was starting high school very soon.

I had a car; I did not have any unserviceable debts. I was a woman who had re-discovered herself. They say everything that happens have already happened before. So, it was inevitable for me to be this person someday. Even more interestingly, I may actually have lived a different life in the past.

This did not happen that easy. I did not become so strong overnight. It was all the huddles we had been through with him.

He may not be here, I know. It hurts me dearly, but I understand. This is what my life was supposed to be. I accept it. I had made some mistakes too that have resulted in this situation, so he says. The main one was the issue with the one thing closest to his heart, my daughter.

At first, I tried to avoid the topic of my daughter's biological father. I felt that it was a chapter that I have dealt with and wanted to leave it in my past. But it happened, this one day, he asked about it. Actually, he would normally ask in passing and take whatever I told dim. This time around I could not lie. I had to tell him the truth. I knew he would understand but I did not know how it would affect us. At this time, I could not accept any problems that would negatively affect our relationship.

The thing with my daughter is a bit complicated. I had a child when I was very young. It was one of those teenager misbehaviour things. I say I was a teenager because I was acting like one but in real age, I was in my early twenties. This guy I had met.

He was all that. He was from a rich family, so I told myself I have hit a jackpot. At the same time, I was also almost going out with another guy. I never really had a relationship with this rich guy. For him, I was a girl from the neighbourhood he wanted to sleep with. So, this one day, I happened to meet him. Not trying to imply anything, I must say, we had sex. Whether consensual sex or not is something that can be left to everyone's interpretation. All I can say is, it was not what I wanted. I cannot say it happened in a heat of a moment or because I could not do anything.

A few months later, I found out that I was pregnant.

It was such an embarrassment to his family that they decided to buy my silence out. They convinced my family that we should get married. In a flash, we got engaged. I moved in with him at his home. Life was going to go on like that. While staying with him, I started seeing where the wealth came from. It was all good. He had me as he had always wanted. We were going to have a child together.

We were going to be a happy family. No one would know the truth on how the child even came about.

Days, weeks, months went by. I was not happy. The idea of me staying with this family for the rest of my life was just not sinking in. I was not one of the most wifely materials those days. You can say I was naughty. Like I have said, I had a lot of male friends and most still wanted me to be with them. Most did not even know I was pregnant. This includes this other guy. The guy I was almost in a relationship with. I started shifting my focus to him while I was working on an exit strategy.

We were close. Some close people knew about him, but I had to make sure that my then new family did not find out.

I finally found a way. This person was a criminal. The only way to get rid of him was to get him arrested. The long and short of it was that I informed on him and that is how he ended up in prison. With him in prison, there was no need for me to stay there. So, I moved out. I went back home. Sometimes I think that this was one of the things that influenced my never normal relationship with my mother.

The pregnancy was starting to show. This guy I was with now knew I was pregnant. We discussed it and we came to an agreement. People could not know that the child belongs to that family. So, he agreed that he would play a shadow father for the child. People now knew him as the father. It was all good and normal until he found someone. He actually found someone I knew very closely. He got married and moved on to a different state. Now we could not keep seeing each other and the wife could not know that the child is said to be his. Him mother believed it and knew that the wife should not know. She thought that it was because we were trying to avoid affecting her son's marriage, but the truth was, if the wife was to find out, we would have to tell the truth. The truth would mean that people would know the biological father. So, we kept it a secret. In my family too, only very few people knew what had happened.

When John came by, he wanted to know the biological father, but again, I was not too honest.

In the months and years of back and forth, I convinced the guy who had been the said father to agree if John asked because John was adamant that he wanted to know. At the time, I did not know why he was so adamant, but he was. One day I told him my version of the story. I told him the reason why the father is not on the picture is because he was married. Well, the guy was married with two kids. So, I was certain that if John ever calls, he would confirm at least that much which means he would believe everything we say. That very same week, I made sure that I get into contact with this guy because John was definitely going to call. I can even remember the conversation that we had. It lasted for a couple of minutes.

"Good Morning Praisey", I wrote

"Hey, how are you doing? I tried to call your cell on Monday. I kept getting your voicemail. By the way, I'm good", he replied

"Hey back at you. Sorry dear, I had a different sim card in my phone. If you want to call, you can call on this number. How was the woman's day?", that was me trying to make small talk.

"Well, it started a bit slow but ended on a high note. How was yours?' he asked.

"Meaning you got some, lol!!!. I slept the whole day, not feeling very good, your brother and I are fighting, interesting neh!", I proceeded trying to warm up the conversation.

By then you should have picked up that all my relationships were based on one thing and one thing only. I allowed men to look at me in a particular way. The results of that are what I am still dealing with to this day.

"I hate to brag every day. I have to shag, as SHAGY will say. As for me I got LUCKY. What was the fight about? Hey, try to loosen up a bit. I'm starting to pick up a trend. You did this with me and now it's my brother. Maybe you need to look at the mirror and see the truth. You are creating these unnecessary fights with him because of your insecurities and if you don't stop, he is going to leave. Nobody wants to be in the court of law everyday where judgement has already been passed. Believe what he tells you and trust me, you will know when he is cheating. Come on, you know you will. How is the little princess doing?" he wrote.

It was a long message. I did not contact him for such. I just wanted to ensure that my plan works out. But what can I say, we had a relationship that was as much of a mess as the one I was in.? I should also explain that Praisey and John were not blood brothers. They did not even know each other. They just shared the same last name. It was like as Hu Fung Li from Hong Kong is not a blood brother to Hu Fung Chin from Beijing, but it can be said that they are brothers through their ancestral lastnames. This was the case with Praisey and John.

"Whatever doctor Phil. It was a pillow fight, lol! She is doing perfectly fine. She had trouble breathing yesterday afternoon. I think it's because she played too much. Nothing serious though. She is fine.

How are my two Angels doing?". The two Angels I referred to were his biological kids from his marriage. My daughter had a heart condition. She would sometimes struggle to breathe. For years, the doctors have managed to do something because the problem has since stopped without undergoing any treatment or operations.

"The guys are fine. The little one gave us a bit of a scare on Monday night, he was just vomiting but now he is OK. The girl is starting to hold us to ransom, she wants a bicycle and I'm worried about her safety because her friends are playing on the street and what if sometimes some drunk just decide to test his car. I know she'll join them as well as much as I'll stress that she must play in the yard. Kids never listen and parents need to be accountable for their mistakes. Well, as for the fight, blood is thinker than water. I'm just looking out for my brother", Dr Phil proceeded. He was always like that. I sometimes think this thing of over analysis is genetic. They are all these same.

"Kids will be kids. What did I ever want with the Hu Fungs. How is work? Please call me in my office", I wrote trying to divert his Dr. Phil tendencies.

"Are you tired of typing? But it supposed to make you look busy. I'll call you", he responded.

"I just wanted to hear your voice and get the whooping while at it…Dr Phil", I said while thinking that at another point in time, this would have meant something totally different.

"Well, I hope to have delivered GOOD service", he closed out.

Praisey always gave good advice. He was that one person who made me forget my baby daddy issues. He still held an important place in my life.

I was going to convince John that Praisey was the biological father of my daughter. This conversation made my life easier. The fact that they were brothers made it even easier. Like he said, blood is thicker than water. So, they would get along. Their egos would also play at my advantage.

Praisey would think that no its fine, I was there first, and John would think, "Well I'm the man now". It was all working out in my favour.

I told John that we had agreed with Praisey that this is how it was going to be. John, being the nice guy he is, he understood. That was the end of. He knew who the father was, and I was content with what I had done. My family was also happy that at least now John knew the truth but yet he is still here so he must have been serious.

Chapter 7

The Family Twist

In the years that followed, we were a happy family. I did not anticipate John ever finding out the truth. I did not even anticipate any possibility of him finding out. What I did not count on were the people out there who would do anything to separate up. This time around, they were there too. Strangely enough, although I do not know who it was, I am certain it was someone very close because John would never listen to anyone, especially when it came to my daughter. Even when he introduced her to his family, it was a matter of "this is my daughter. I didn't want to bother bringing her when she was still younger because it would have made no difference anyway". That was it. To date it still baffles me who might have given him a different version of what I had given. Somehow, he found out because he would not have asked me again if he had not received any alternative information. He knew I lied. I could not tell him the truth again. How do I explain to someone like him that I was protecting a criminal? John hated absent fathers. I think it had to do with his own father issues. How would he take it that I lied, and his own brother also lied to him about such an important thing? It would have shattered him.

Even worse, when this question came up, we were not in a good space. I was not certain whether we were not in a good space because of what he had found out or being not in a good space resulted in him digging the truth.

One day, he asked me to explain what happened again. I was sure he wanted to dig holes in my story. I stuck to it.

I remembered it word by word. Although he never said anything, I could see in his eyes that he did not believe me. I was ready for him to come out with it, but alas, he was quiet as always as if he was upset. That was the one thing that was frustrating about him. When he was upset, he would just keep quiet. He would say "what's the point of arguing about something because a person does whatever they do because they think it's the right thing to do". Who was he to say otherwise?

The lies continued until this day. The day that changed my life forever. This time, it was not for the better. It was starting to become my worst nightmare. Everything I had worked so hard to protect was crumbling right in front of my eyes. I could not even remember what happened that day or what he asked or said. All I know is that he knew that the biological father was in prison, and he was back. He knew that I had been seeing him without his knowledge. I do not know how he knew, but whatever happened it might have happened when this guy picked me up somewhere to go to the mall. The strange part is that since I was trying to protect everyone, I made sure that he did not pick me up from anywhere close to home.

I suspect that John may have seen me getting into this guy's car. It was possible. John was wherever he wanted to be when he wanted to be. He may have known about it or found out from my phone conversation since at some point I know John had access to my phone through whatever software he was using.

He was pissed. I saw it in his eyes that he was pissed off. Mostly it was the disappointment that hurt more than being upset. To him, it meant that I did not trust him enough to tell him the truth. After close to a decade together, it meant that I did not trust him enough. I did not trust what he said about my daughter. I made him just another father. I knew he would emotionally punish me one way or another.

I felt it in my spine that this maybe it. I could not get myself to feel anything. I was numb. My whole body was numb. Maybe this was it. Maybe not. I still had faith. Faith is what has kept me this long. Faith was what had kept us this long. This time around though, it all felt hopeless.

It then donned on me. How would he have found out

the truth? Was it something I said or did? Was it because I have been seeing my daughter's biological father behind his back? But he was far, how would he know that. Obviously, some nosey being may have told him. I wondered who that might be. What did they expect to gain from all this? Maybe it was one of his floozy's. He has sure banged a number of them in my neighbourhood. Well, that's what I believe although he has always denied it all. I was numb.

One part of me was worried about what he may know while another part was recalling all the lies, he had told before. It was not like I was the only one with hidden skeletons. If the rumours had anything to do with it, he sure had a couple of skeletons too. The truth was, although I never felt any less of a woman being with him, sometimes his actions made me feel like I was not worthy. I sometimes felt like I always had to be perfect while he could be whatever he wanted to be as and when he felt like it. There were a lot of memories that started coming back. These were things I did not want to remember, but there I was, instead of worrying about the future, I was worried about the past, about what John had done to me and I was trying to find something to make myself feel better about the whole thing.

This other time, there was this girl he referred to as a sister when I asked. She was like a sister he never had, he would say.

I was not certain at what point did he first meet her. All I remember was that he had met her somewhere close to where he was staying. She stayed in the same neighborhood. He used to say she was like his sister. Knowing John, there could be no such thing. To him, a woman was for one thing and one thing only. That thing was definitely not something that would just stick around because she was being called a sister. They used to spend a lot of time together. At some point, I remember someone telling me that she had seen them at the mall. John never went to the malls.

The fact that he could take this girl out meant that there was something much more than just a sisterly love.

She never helped the situation either. First, she did not like me. To be exact, she hated me. Secondly, she did not like the relationship I had with John. To be precise, she hated it. She used to tell people that she did not understand what John saw in me. To her, I was just a slut hanging on to John. She felt that John deserved better. Every time I would confront John about it, he would just brush it off as just rumours. The one thing I never understood was when one day I asked him to choose between me and her and he, in not so many words, chose her. At the time, I was very angry with him. I was wondering how he could choose her over me if she was just a sisterly friend. I had to suck it up and move on with my life while pretending as if she did not exist. The most hurtful part was that we were both working in the same company which meant that we would bump into each other on more occasions than one.

Come to think of it, John would never choose a girl over another unless he felt that he had nothing to lose. In this case, many years later I found out that they actually were just friends. Although I could not understand why he would have chosen her over me, but I later learnt that with John, he would rather lose a relationship than a friendship. He would say that if a person wants to leave, they should be free to do so. He always said that this girl was the only girl who liked him, but nothing ever happened.

He may have liked her too but had decided at an early stage that he would friend-zone her. Everything that followed was about him helping her finish her internship. Although they were not in the same department, John was well versed with the other departments so he could help.

He used to proofread her reports and help her in a

number of projects she was doing. He was also her middleman between her level and the management level. John sat on the review board, so he knew how each mentor presented their interns. In this case, John used to prepare her for presentations based on whatever concerns her mentor had raised. He also would randomly check her training progress against the requirements of her mentor and let her know where she needed to improve.

In short, this was just one of those moments where I may have blamed other people for my insecurities. All the memories of everything and every detail were flashing in front of me. Joh was never that perfect, but I could not fault him on things based on just rumors.

Another moment was this other colleague of ours. It was a similar story to that of his so-called sister. The truth is, I never really found any proof before accusing him of cheating on me with her. I actually listened to someone who was not even my friend. She had claimed that John was seen dropping off this colleague at some town nearby. First, it did not make sense to me. I knew he may have had a thing for her, but I had never seen them together.

For me, it was easy to pick up those who had a thing for him; they all had one thing in common. They would all suddenly be over friendly with me, or they would suddenly hate me for no apparent reason. Those who would become over-friendly would do so, so that maybe if we see John, it would not be awkward if they start mumbling about something. People who are doing something behind your back would always try to be overly open around you. They would want to make you feel as if they are just friends with your partner so that you do not start noticing or thinking other things when you see them together. The lady was one of those who became overly nice to me so when I heard that he was seen with her, I flipped. This time around I was not going to take that lying down. I was going to fight it to the end.

I may have overreacted, but I had to tell someone. Unfortunately, the person I told ended up telling others until it got to the wrong people.

The day it all broke loose, I remember that John was not at work. I tried calling him, but he did not pick up. The story was that the person I had told decided to report the matter to the management team. I did not know what she said but it became a big issue that this girl was involved with John. On that particular day, she had already completed her training and was awaiting her permanent appointment. The paperwork had started as the month when she was supposed to start on had already started. Normally after your internship, you leave site if there is no permanent appointment.

However, with her, she was going to be appointed. It was just that the human capital management department had delayed. She was then asked to carry on working while the paperwork was still being sorted out.

Unfortunately for her, all the drama unfolded on the day when she was supposed to sign her permanent appointment. After she had heard that I complained to someone about her and John, she came to confront me. Now that is one thing no one should ever do. I may be a nice person, but I had my limits. That day, those limits were pushed to the edge. The only person who could resolve that matter was not around. He was not going to be around for a whole week from that day so the matter could not be addressed. Instead of trying to resolve the issue, her management team decided not to proceed with her appointment. Her internship contract had lapsed in any way so she could not remain on site without a contract. She was asked to vacate the premises and that was the end of her career with our organization. I do not know what happened between her and John afterwards, but I sure know that I did not have to deal with her at work anymore. She was gone.

Many years later it had surfaced that the lady who had told me about her had actually lied. That Friday when it was alleged that John was seen with her in town was all a made-up story.

What had happened was that John being John, he liked women any way, so he did not mind driving with one, whom he had a crush on and knew very well that she also liked him that way, he had decided to give her a lift. The girl had asked for a lift from him after work because her normal transport (her baby daddy) had an emergency. Because John knew that people were already speculating about them being in a relationship, he could not pick her up from the parking lot, so he had asked this other lady to drop her off somewhere on the way then John could pick her up there and drop her off in town. That was exactly what happened. As it turned out, he did not even take her to town, he dropped her off just outside town where her baby daddy was going to pick her up.

For my case, maybe I should have asked myself if that lady had been truthful, what she was doing in that town anyway because it was a town that she never went to. Maybe I should have asked her where about exactly she saw them because she did not even know that town that well. I guess I can say that I had been fighting the same fight for years, so I did not need any confirmation when it came to John and these women.

These were not the only two. There were also rumours regarding this other one who was very close to me. First, I knew she was going out with one of John's colleagues. One day, his colleague came to me and complained that John was taking his girl. Obviously, I would believe him.

That fight also went on for some time until I had no energy to deal with it.

As it turned out, it was well far-fetched from the truth. John had had an argument with his colleague the day before. He had always been one to hit you where it matters the most. This girl had just started working with us. Knowing how guys there were like, everyone was hoping to be the first guy in. John's colleague had already scored.

He was the king of the jungle. He was tapping the new girl on the in the office. That was the guys' game.

This one day he had an argument with John about something. John being John, he knew that this guy's girlfriend, the new girl, would be in town that weekend. John called to check where this guy was, the guy confirmed that he was going to town. Remember, John already stayed in town by that time. The next thing was that he called this girl. Well, he told her that he knew she was in town and waiting for her boyfriend by the name of so and so. She disputed it because she did not want to be seen as that girl who just started work and now was having affairs at work. The forever convincing John asked to meet with her if she was alone. She could not change and say she was not alone, so she agreed. At the time, they were not even close so to her it would take a couple of minutes and then she would proceed with her plans. John was just a guy she knew from work, and she knew him as her boyfriend's colleague.

Few minutes passed, a lot of minutes passed, and it turned to hours. No one would ever know what happened or what they did or did not do that day.

While she was with John, she could not pick up the phone because she thought that John would see the name on the call list and start asking too many questions. She just switched off her phone. John's friend knew how John operated and he knew that he had always joked about this girl. When she was no longer picking up his calls, he concluded that she might have been with John.

He called John and John claimed to be in his flat. He wanted to take another friend and come and visit John, and then John flip-flopped. He claimed that he was leaving for the South for something urgent. Even after the guy had insisted that he was already in town, John refused to see him. The next moment, John's phone was no longer ringing; this girl's phone was also no longer ringing. The colleague then concluded that they were together. The only way he could get revenge was to tell on him. John did not care.

At the time, we were on and off so he did not care what this guy would do, and he knew exactly what he would do. John actually came to me before this guy came with some shady story. I cannot remember what he said exactly but whatever it was, he made sure that I did not believe his colleague's story.

The one incident that I could never forgive John for was in relation to this other colleague. Yes, because John did not have too many friends or any friends at all and he spent most of his time at work, he was always rumoured to be having an affair with one of the other employees.

There were so few women in our site that almost all of them were rumoured to be in a relationship with him at one point or the other. This girl was very cheeky. She used to rub it in that she had been to his apartment. I never knew whether it was true or not, but she sounded very convincing. Her entire department seemed to know about it. I guess she could not shut her mouth after opening her legs for someone's boyfriend. Maybe she thought she had achieved something. Maybe to her, it was some sort of an achievement to sleep with John. I admit though, according to him, sleeping with him was. Cheeky bastard.

It all started back in the days when I still had not made up my mind about John. I did not know this until very late in our relationship. Although she had claimed that they were going out, John had always disputed it. I cannot take sides though because at some point, he did ask me what I expected him to do while I was still making up my mind which took over a year. That statement meant that maybe the rumours were true. But they could not have been true because this girl had a known boyfriend at work that happened to be very close to John. Well, knowing John, that would not deter him, instead, he would actually like it that way since there would be no attachments. He hated that. He hated people who got attached. He would rather do other people's girlfriends than find a decent girl to be with.

Maybe that is why he was with me. He had taken me from someone he respected, and he knew that I was not the overly-attached type. He could pretend as if he did not know me for a whole week, until he wanted to see me.

All these things had built up a certain anger in me. There was a time when I also wanted to experience what he was experiencing. I wanted to experience people gossiping about me and see how he would take it. That was what led me to his other brother. Once again, it was not his biological brother by birth, but they shared the same last name.

I had been on and off with this guy before but ever since John, I had put the on and off scenario on a permanent pause. That time, I just had to press the play button, and everything would fall into place. So, I did. The unfortunate part was that I was so vested in John that I could not even enjoy that fling. Before I knew it, John had found out. In not so many words, he instructed me to end it or go. By that time, I had broken up with John eleven times. I remember that because he used to count. He had always said the dozenth time would be the final end. So, I did, I broke up with this guy.

I was still very much in love with John. Other relationships did not make sense. So, I committed. He also was finding his feet again. He was becoming the loyal boyfriend I had always painted him out to be. It was never about how people looked at him though, for me, it was about knowing that I had a one-woman man. I understood that one way to get him loyal was not to allow him time to wonder around but allow him to be himself. That was when I decided that even if he were to come at midnight, I would give him what he wanted.

In that case, it was safe for me, safe for him and good for our relationship. I was becoming his wife. I was his wife. I was his unmarried wife.

Chapter 8

The Truth Shall Set You Free

It was clear that something had happened. At the time, I did not know what and how exactly. But as time went by, I was made to believe, or should I say, I concluded that it was someone very close to me. I swear it was her. They go way back. At some point I could swear there was something going on between them.

She was just a girl I knew from the neighbourhood. We were not very close then. We just knew each other. The first time John saw her, I knew he would fall for her. They met at his workplace. She had been working there for some time and John was new. John had a problem, I must admit. To him, every beautiful woman around him should bow down to him, if not be his. I cannot say be his girlfriend because he never considered them as such. He would just say, "They are people I get along with".

This one day, he had come down to work at her workplace. We were in the same organization, just different sites.

It was a lovely day. John was in one of his good moods, which is something that did not happen too often. Joy was also in one of her ever-happy moods.

Apparently, from the details I was made privy to, John did not even greet her when they first met. He just looked at her and walked past. She was not very impressed. She was actually livid. Who the hell is this guy, she thought? Why wouldn't he greet when he meets new people. Unfortunately, as it turned out, out of all the people John met that day, she was the only one he did not greet.

It was one of his psychological approaches he used with women. The fact that everyone on site who met this guy thought he was a cool guy; she would never forget his face. She would always wonder why not her. That is exactly what John wanted.

On that day, John was with one of his colleagues. This colleague knew Joy from the neighbourhood. Everyone around John seemed to know each other. He was just the only outsider.

A day or two went by and nothing of that meeting came up. John did not seem to have paid any interest to this lady. Maybe I should say that he pretended not to, but deep down he knew he wanted her. He could not ask his colleague because he did not want his colleague to know. The one thing John always avoided was to know the person's past. He claimed that people are people. There could never be a person who could grow up without mistakes just because they are waiting for him. He was an adult now and adult people become adults by going through life. They experience different things in life.

To him, knowing a person's past introduces either an element of judgement before even getting to know the person or an element of ignorance on how he would approach that person. He preferred to go in blank. Well, he enjoyed going in blank in me as well. In this context though, I mean, he preferred to meet a person without digging their past. He wanted to approach a person with an objective mind. The rest would be revealed as time went by.

In the case of Joy, well, she was beautiful. She was an adult. Obviously, she had slept around once or twice. Maybe even million times, who knows? That was something he did not want to know. As guys, he knew that the first thing a guy would tell you about a girl the other guy is interested in is who she was with. He did not care and did not want to know. So, he never asked.

One day his colleague told him that Joy had complained how arrogant John was. She had asked why he couldn't just greet her like any other person. This was it. She had paid attention to him. She remembered him. There was something she hated about him. Well, that was his entry point.

There was something in common they could talk about when they meet again. He could play along and claim that he did greet her, and she did not respond. Or he could claim that maybe she did not hear him. Either way, this would introduce a sense of relief for Joy. She would feel that maybe it was her who did not hear him. She would maybe even feel bad about why she didn't at least greet him if she actually believed that he had not greeted her.

She would finally blame herself for that day. It would be maybe it was her fault that throughout the day, John never said anything. It would have been because he had greeted her, and she did not respond. He was probably upset with her. He is a very soft-spoken person so maybe he was not audible enough but at least he did greet; she just did not hear him.

John did not want the colleague to know that he had paid any attention to Joy so he pretended as if he did not remember the girl being spoken about. That was as far as the conversation had gone. John was hoping that his colleague would go back and tell Joy that John did not even remember her. This would shatter her feelings. She was beautiful so she knew that every guy who saw her would at least remember her. Let alone a guy who spent the whole day around her, probably bumping into each other more than 30 times just that day. She would start asking herself thousand questions. But then, she would want to show this guy what he did not see. She would be looking forward to meeting him again and this time she would make sure that he notices her. Her hope would be that this arrogant guy would have an interest in her and she would brush him off.

She would want him to regret never paying any attention the first time around. That would be her revenge approach.

Weeks went by. Months went by. Nothing in relation to that day ever came up again until John's colleague reminded John of that girl who said he was arrogant and full of himself.

The colleague had just met Joy over the weekend and the topic came up again. Well, John is full of himself, that is a given. Ask anybody who knows him to describe him, and they would not leave out how full of himself he is. To him, it is not arrogance; it is just a lack of self-doubt. That is how he puts it.

This time around, John told his colleague that they should go back there and see this lady. He knew his colleague would tell that to Joy. As planned, his colleague did. Joy was excited. This guy was coming back. He was coming back just for me. She did not know how to take it. Should she be nice to him to show him how good of a person she was, shall she be rude to him because of what she thought he had done? Joy was in limbo. She looked forward to the day they come back but did not know how that day would go. First thing, John had very sharp eyes. What if he just stands there and stirs at her. What would she say? Greet? Walk away? Smile? Frown? what exactly would she do. Or what should she do.

The day came. John took his colleague to where Joy worked. It was part of the same organization so there were no red tapes on access etc. John's position anyway allowed him to go wherever he wanted within the organization. He was an intern so during training, the Interns need to understand all spheres of the business. This trip was no different. On paper that is. It was just a normal trip where John would want to go and observe something at this site.

Joy knew he was coming. She dressed up in one of her favorite work wear. She looked over her mirror million times that morning. She wanted to be in her best. She wanted this guy to regret ever ignoring her the first time he came by. The question still stood though, it stood until John arrived, how should Joy react? That question was never answered and as it turned out, it did not matter. John was the very same John she had met that first time. He was forever grumpy towards her but friendly to everyone else.

As they were walking in from the gate, Joy saw them. She made sure that she stands where they would definitely go past her. She wanted to see if he would greet this time around or what he would do this time around.

As they walked in, John met other Joy's colleagues. He greeted them with a smile and had a small chats with them. This was getting interesting. John was in a good mood, Joy thought. She also got excited. "Damn, this guy is not that bad looking just has a bad attitude", she talked to herself. Here he was, standing right in front of her. He stood so close you could swear they were close friends, and he was going to go for a hug. She stood there, trying to wipe the smile off her face. She looked at him, he looked at her. John turned around to look at his colleague. "Is this her?" he asked his colleague. His colleague responded by affirming that indeed it was her. John took a step back. Looked at her from head to toes and from toes to head, he gave her one of his infamous smacky-smiles and said "well, she's beautiful". Then he walked away.

Joy was livid. She was furious. She was boiling. She could not believe that this guy just did what he did. Who the hell did he think he was? She was confused. Was she not his type maybe? What was the deal with this guy? In her head though, that voice was still lingering "well, she's beautiful". He had at least said something. He still did not greet; he still did not say anything directly to her.

During lunch time, John and his colleague went to where Joy was having lunch. John just walked up and told her he needed a cup of coffee. No, he did not request her to make him one, he demanded her with that tone to make him one. Joy looked around; everyone around the table seemed not to notice anything wrong with this. Instead, while she was still seating there, the older women stared at Joy "the man has spoken" one of them said. Joy respected all these women so she could not say no to John's request in front of them. She stood up, took a cup out of the cabinet. "Coffee or Tea", she asked. "Coffee with two sugars and milk", John responded. Joy made the coffee, gave it to him and John thanked her and walked out.

The ladies around the table, as always, ladies always gossip about everything, started speculating that Joy maybe knew this guy from somewhere, if not, this guy liked her or maybe she even liked him too. Joy refuted all those utterances. She maintained that this guy is just arrogant and had no respect for her. He did not even greet her when he first came here and today, he also did not greet her but yet demanded coffee from her. Deep down, she was happy. At least they were talking.

Maybe the ladies were right. Maybe this guy liked her or maybe she herself liked him. Only time would tell.

Throughout the rest of the day, they never bumped into each other.

It was not because they were working at different stations; it was because Joy made sure that she avoided him as much she could. It was until that afternoon that they bumped into each other again. This time around, Joy had no other option. John was standing close to the exit door, and it was home time for everyone. Joy had to go through that door. So, she did.

As she walked by, John moved closer to her, blocking her path. "So, by the way, my name is John, and you are?" he asked, once again with his forever serious face. Joy felt her knees shaking. While she was contemplating on how to address this matter, she found herself responding "I'm Joy". "Well, I can see its home time, so I will let you go. I will call you tomorrow on your office line", John said while moving out of her way. "Let me go?" Joy asked herself. Does this guy mean to tell me that my going home had anything to do with him? I was going home anyway, so why would he claim that he was the one who was letting her go. Joy was getting upset. She was thinking if this guy wants to say something to her, why he can't just go ahead instead of all these games. She looked at him and walked away.

She clocked out as usual, got into her transport and went home. That whole evening and part of the night, she could not stop thinking about John. John who? Who cares? He's cool though, just arrogant.

The following day, Joy could not leave her office, hoping John would call as promised. The day went by; nothing much mattered for Joy that day. All she wanted was that call. She did not even know what the call is for, but she wanted that call to come through. Every time the phone rang, her heart would beat a little bit faster, only to be shattered by the voice on the other side. It was not until that afternoon, just before she went home. The phone rang. Once, twice, and three times. She took a deep breathe. Picked up the phone. It was him. He actually called.

"Hi", he first spoke.

"Hi", Joy responded.

"Well, how is you", John asked.

"I'm fine thanks, how are you?" Joy responded trying to stay as calm as she could.

"Oh, I see, well, I'll get straight to the point. I know you are not fine; you are actually over the mood that I called. I know you wish I was there with you, and I am sure you wouldn't mind that. So, when are you coming to my place?" John asked.

There was silence on Joy's side. She did not know what to say. She just could not take this treatment anymore. This guy was too much.

"Did you just ask me to come to your place?" Joy asked with a deep voice.

I am not sure whether she was trying to intimidate him

or what. Intimidate who, John? John was not the type to get intimidated that easily.

"Wait my sister, I was not opening a conversation about it, I am just asking you when are you coming to my place?" John interjected when he felt that she was trying to ask too many questions. Joy did not respond.

"Well, I will call to finalise the date with you. What is your mobile number?" he asked.

Joy gave him her mobile number. He thanked her and put down the phone. Joy packed up and went home all confused, excited, angry, upset, happy, and all the other feelings you can think off.

Once again, a few days went by. It was coming up to a weekend. That Friday, John called again. Joy picked up. They chatted a bit. Joy refused to go to John's place that weekend, but they agreed that someday they would make a plan.

That was the beginning of their crazy relationship. Sometimes they were friends, sometimes they would appear as if they were in a relationship, sometimes they would appear as if they were family, but throughout, they were very close. It was also not a hidden secret that Joy did not like the relationship I had with John. She never directly said it, but I know she did not. So, it would not surprise me if I were to find out that she was the one who saw me with my daughter's biological father and told John.

In any way, I still do not know how, but I know someone did. My life was hanging in limbo. I did not know what our relationship with John would be like after that event. He now knew the truth and he hated that it was kept from him for that long. I was wrong, I must admit.

If I could turn back the time, I would but unfortunately life does not work like that. During all that time, I had been a wife to him, he had been my husband, and nothing was going to change that.

Chapter 9

The Day Joy May Have Seen

It was a lovely day. The sun was shining bright. The sea breeze was hovering over the skies. The sky was blue. Birds were singing. The neighbour's dog was hissing under the shade. There was a cat sitting over the fence. It had been sitting there for hours now. Every time birds sat next to it; it would appear as if it wanted to jump on them but yet it just sat there. I think it was exhausted from the heat of the sun. It was also full. I had just given it a bowl of milk and some biscuits. Yes, our cat ate fancy. It never ate any leftovers like some cats I've seen. It only ate cat food, meat, biscuits and drank milk. I guess it was a sophisticated type of a cat.

My daughter was at school. My sister had gone shopping. My mother had gone to work. My brother had also gone to work. I was alone. I was going to leave for work soon. I had an afternoon shift. I had already taken a bath, a cold one too because of this heat outside. I was all dressed up. Because of the heat, I had my hat ready for the sun. I was about to leave the house when my phone rang. I looked at it. I had not seen that number for some time. It was just saved as "Him". Obviously, it was a guy. It was a guy I used to know. Well, a guy I still know. I hesitated a bit but picked it up anyway.

"Hi", I answered.

"Hi to you too", a deep voice responded.

He started talking and I just listened. By this time, I was already outside. I had locked the house, taken the keys to my neighbour and ready to leave.

I normally left the key at my neighbours if there is no one around so that my daughter could get into the house when she came back from school. Leaving the keys there was also a "good-to-do" act. It was always safer that way. Imagine if you had left a water tap running and the neighbour sees water coming from the doorway but have no keys to come and check what was happening, they would be helpless. That was why we left the key there. Obviously, all the elders in the house had their own spare keys, just my daughter. She was still young.

The sun was heating my head like braai coal heating a thick layer of pork ribs. I was boiling. My transport to work used to pick me up about a mile from my house. Normally, I could handle the walk. It was good for my body. It was good for this sexy body. It kept my energy high. That day, I just did not feel like walking that long. I knew I was still early so I could walk slowly. But I was just not feeling it. My feet would ache. I was wearing flat shoes. I only wore flat shoes at work because I could not wear high heels. At least with high heels, I could walk for a distance. I think I trained my feet to be used to high heels. I always tried higher and higher. John liked them, so I had to always have high heels when he sees me and that was almost every day. He said they turned him on.

I never understood it, but I knew that my posture and walk changed when I was on high heels. Maybe he enjoyed seeing me walk in them. Well, I was a catwalk material anyway. I could have made it in the modelling industry if I were not this short. I am about 1.55m and I heard that models should be at least 1.7m or taller, so I did not even bother to try it. But I can sure walk on heels.

The guy over the phone was talking about coming to see me. I think he was already on his way though because he kept on asking if I was at home and I told him I was already walking to my transport.

While walking out the gate, I was still on the phone with him. Before I knew it, the car drove up the driveway. He hung up the phone and turned the vehicle to face the other direction towards where I was heading. I locked the gate, got into the car and he started driving. We greeted each other and started talking. He told me what he was there for and offered to take me to work. That was a big

"NO".

I could never be seen with this guy. My mother would probably drop dead if she were to see us together. This guy had given a lot of stress to me and my family. I just could not be seen being brought by him to work. I declined the offer and asked him to drop me off where my transport would pick me up. He seemed to agree.

When we approached the bus stop, he asked if I was prepared to stand in the sun as he did not mind waiting with me. I agreed for him to wait.

A second later, I realized that this was as bad as him taking me to work. The people in that bus would see us together and start asking questions.

My mother would know. Some of these people knew this guy. Some knew our history so it would not be a good idea to be seen by them with him. Damn, that was turning out to get complicated. While I was thinking what to do, he offered to drive me further down the street. He said he would stop when he sees the bus and drop me off wherever the bus would be. Before I could even answer, he started driving again. We were heading in a different direction. I did not mind because it was still early so, he would still catch the bus. We drove and drove. Nothing much was said. The stereo was playing soft music. The guy seemed distant. He was not the person I last saw. He looked different. He appeared to be deep in thoughts. I let him be as I was also busy chatting with some colleagues on my phone.

All along while I was busy on my phone, I was not looking at where we were going. When the vehicle stopped, I looked up. We were in front of his gate. My heart started racing. Why were we there? I had bad experiences with that place. This was where my whole life changed. That was where that day had all begun many years ago. I was there. The gate was opening, we drove in. "I just need to pick something up", he said.

He went inside. I waited. I waited and waited. The bus

time was getting close. I had to leave. We were too far from the bus stop then and I could not walk that distance.

Even if I tried, I would miss the bus. I walked out of the car towards the house to go and call him. He saw me coming and just ignored me. As I approached, his mother was there.

She greeted and asked a few things and walked out. She closed the gate behind her. Now it was just the two of us standing in front of the house. I wanted to leave.

"You should call in sick", he said.

I refused. I told him I saw no reason to. After so many years and so much stress he had put me through, I should then just call in sick just because he says so. No, I would not do that. I refused.

He walked into the house and sat down. I stood there just outside the door. He asked me to come in. After trying to refuse for some time, I went in and sat opposite him. The sun outside was not helping. I could not walk to the bus stop, I could not stand there bathing under the sun, I could not sit in the vehicle because it was also getting too hot, so I went in. I sat there. We did not say much to each other. Some memories of the past came back. I was a stronger person then. The hatred cannot stay forever. I was a bigger person. I would not allow him to intimidate me. I was older and wiser then. I could make my own decisions. That was all I was thinking about. I did not know what he was thinking about, and I did not care.

To this day, I cannot tell what happened but all I know is that one thing led to another. I called in sick so the bus would not wait for me and ended up spending the entire afternoon with him. Yes, we did. We had sex right there is the seating room. It was the first time after almost a decade. It was different. This time I wanted to. Or should I say, this time I had a choice whether to say yes or no but somehow, I chose not to say no. It happened. It just happened. I cannot say whether it was good or not.

John had taught me things no one could ever do so I

could never really compare him to anyone. He was in a league of his own. This was just sex, nothing more, nothing less. It meant something though.

I did not know what it was, but it was something. Maybe I had forgiven him. Maybe I was just being a slut. I do not know.

As the evening went by, we started talking about our past life. He wanted to be part of my daughter's life. He wanted me to introduce her to him, to his family and he wanted to start supporting her again. He said his mother wanted to have a relationship with her granddaughter and I should not deprive her of that. It was not her who made all those mistakes so she should not be punished for it. I did not know how to react. We had just seemed to consummate our relationship. Whatever it was. So, I was confused. I needed the money for my child, and he sure could provide.

I eventually agreed but told him it would be under my terms. I had to try and explain to my daughter why John is suddenly not the father. She would be shattered. She was young, yes, but she was as strong as hell. She may actually understand it or maybe not. However, we agreed that I would work on it. He gave me some money, claiming to be for my daughter and we walked out.

It was already late. I knew my mother was not back home yet. It was time for people returning from work, so the streets were busy. I did not want my mother to ask me too many questions, so I asked him to drop me off somewhere far from home. I was going to walk. The sun had subsided so I would manage.

When we arrived where he was going to drop me off, the bus from my company had also just arrived. I could not leave his vehicle until everyone from that bus has left the vicinity. We waited. People went by. One by one, they went by. Some looked towards us, some just walked past as if they did not even notice the vehicle parked there.

Few minutes later, the street was quiet again. I said my

goodbyes and left his vehicle. I walked home. My mother was there. I told her I was not feeling well and had to comeback from the bus stop. She did not ask too many questions. I took a shower and afterwards carried on with my normal chores as always when I am at home. That would include cooking, cleaning and feeding the dogs and the cat. Well, feeding the dogs was not really my chore as such but I just enjoyed it.

My daughter returned from school as any other day. We laughed and chatted about all the silly things we always chat about but this time around things were different. Every time I looked at her, I imagined all the possibilities of how was I going to introduce this other father to her? I wondered how she would take it. Would she accept him? Would she hate John? Would she be upset with me? Would this affect her schoolwork? All those thoughts frightened me. After this long, I now had to deal with this again. How would I tell John all about this? I had lied to him for years. My family had always thought John knew everything. Now it was this. I had to undo what I had done many years ago.

How would my family take it? I was getting frightened. I shrugged it off. The day went by. We all went on with our normal lives as if nothing had happened.

It was not until John called and asked me questions about my daughter that it struck me. He would not have asked if nothing new had happened. Somebody told him something and this time it sounded like he knew the truth because he was not really asking, he was telling me that my lies have resulted to this. He wanted clarity. He wanted confirmation of whatever he knew. The question was what had happened. It donned me. Somebody must have seen me with the other guy that day. Somebody must have seen me leaving his vehicle that day. It must have been somebody who was on the bus or had left the bus that day. Out of everyone who was there, only one person could have bothered to tell John. I had always known that she never approved of our relationship. The problem was that she probably would have had to explain to him who this guy was. This person knew me from my past. She knew the guy we fronted with as the biological father, and she knew that it was not true. She had suspected that this guy I was with was the biological father. With me being seen with him, it must have given her confirmation. She might have just told John everything. Sometimes I felt like she had always wanted John for herself. The only thing that stopped her was when they found out that they were related. If it was not for that, they would probably be together. With John being John, I would not be surprised if I were to ever hear that he actually slept with her before finding out that they were related.

He probably even knew that just before they slept together but carried on with it and claimed that he did not know. If that was the case, then they have a bond no one can ever break.

They say in such occurrences, it takes a miracle to separate such people.

That was the beginning of the end. That was the point where I felt that I had just lost him. I had no choice but to tell him everything. He was upset. Actually, more disappointed than upset. I believe that it was through Joy that he found out the truth. From that day onwards, I had to work extra hard to keep him. All along, all I had to do was to service him well and he would forget all my mistakes and shortfalls. This time around, it felt like nothing would ever work. He started feeling very distant. He would not call as often as he used to. He would use one-word answers when I talk to him. He was no longer himself. I felt him slipping through my figure tips. He even took out the ring he had worn for some years which made people believe that we had actually secretly gotten married. I tried my best to rebuild what we had, what we have and what we will always have. He was still my husband, and I was still his wife. My commitment to him had not changed. I was still his UnMarried Wife.

Chapter 10

The Day I Died

Early morning one day, couple of months after the whole incident took place, John called to tell me he was coming to see me. The excitement was uncontrollable. It had always been like this ever since he moved further far from our city. Every time he came down, we would have our best times ever. Sometimes though I felt that he was just trying to punish me for what I had done. He would come around the time I could not be intimate with him. He knew that it is the one thing that had kept us thus far.

This time around, it was the perfect timing. I had started gym again. I was feeling younger, healthier and sexier than ever before. I was also on a mission to prove people wrong that since he had left, he would also leave me. I was in a mission to prove whoever told him about the truth that we were meant for eternity. I was excited that he was coming. I planned a dinner date the day he would arrive. We were going to go out to the beach, have dinner under the skyline at one of my favorite restaurants near the beach. Afterwards we would go to the lighthouse and do what we once did there one New Year's night day. I felt like I had to remind him of what we had always had. I wanted him to come back.

I wanted him to get a job close by and come back. Maybe we would have more kids, get married and live happily ever after. I knew he did not want to talk about marriage. He actually hated the term "marriage". But I had always had faith. I had always had hope that someday, we would get married.

I still do have hope. It is the only thing that keeps me going. Sometimes apart from my daughter, it is the only thing that keeps me breathing. I love this man. He may not care much but I know he knew I love him. He was coming to visit. It was going to be a great weekend.

Late afternoon on his day of arrival, he called, "I'm outside" as usual. We went to him. All excited, me and my daughter. We greeted him and he greeted back. He started asking about school and all the other things he always asked my daughter. It was well and good. We were all happy. It was getting late. My daughter went back to the house. We stayed in the car. As always, strange things happened in the car. It had become like a cult. It was like he could not listen to anything without certain things happening first. It was my duty to make him happy. He had driven a very long distance, so he needed to distress. So, I obliged without him asking. A few hours later, suddenly the mood became tense. These moments do happen now and again but that day, it felt even heavier. I sat there and waited. I was waiting for him to tell me we can go. I waited, waited and waited and it never came. Instead, a short speech started:

"Luv Luv, we have been through a lot together. We have come up tops.

A lot of people did not anticipate that we would be here today, and some even tried their best to separate us. I have trusted you over everything people have been saying. I had done that for years. I know you have also been through a lot regarding the things people claim I do and yes most of them were true, but some were not. I could go on and on one by one, but it would not change anything now. Instead of me going through all the heartaches we have been through; let me get straight to the point. I met someone. I always meet people, but you should know that I am telling you about this one because it is serious. I am getting married. We are getting married. She will be my wife very soon. Yes, we have not been together for that long. Actually, we do not know each other at all. We just met but we are getting married. I would like to keep the relationship with my daughter, but it all depends on you. I do understand how this would make you feel but that is what is going to happen. I know some people may think that I am making a mistake. Well, if that's the case, it would be my mistake. I would deal with it my way and I don't expect anyone to comment. I told my family the same thing. I do not expect them to comment. I was telling them not asking for their advice that I am getting married. I know this would shatter you, so I guess there is no need for me to be here anymore. So let me go. We would talk. Try and keep calm and enjoy the rest of your evening. I shall see you around. I will come by before I leave. Just so you know, I do not think I will ever find someone who would love me like you have done, let alone someone who would fulfil all my fantasies like you can.

You will always be the best. Judging by the current situation, no, she is not any better. She will not even love me for who I am but somehow, I think she's the one. There is something about her that made me take this decision. And no, even her family does not approve so it may not even work out. It is just what it is. I will always hold you dearly to my heart. You have been there for me even when I had no one. You have saved me from a lot of human dangers. I know I was not the best you deserved. Life is what it is. We all have to be strong. Damn, you are by far the best. If you are wondering if maybe it was the sex that took me, well, no, she is nowhere close to you. Actually, she is nowhere close to what I've experienced in general. When it compares to you, I would say if you were a 100, she would be a 30. So, no, it was not that. Is she more educated? No, not at all. She claims to be studying but I don't see any prospects. Is she rich? No, even you have a better account balance than her. Is she more sexier or beautiful? No, she is average and definitely you have a banging body so she can't be sexier than you. She is just ordinary. I have never thought about marriage, so I think the fact that I am thinking about it now, then I think that it's the right thing to do".

That was it. He gave it with a straight face. I could see that he did not expect me to make any comments. For over an hour, we stayed there. We sat there. Nothing was spoken. My world had just crumbled right in front of my own eyes. It was all over. I was done. We were done. Him? getting married? that was it.

He would now have a wife. He would probably have kids with her. I would no longer be his wife. I had always been his wife, although not married, but I was always his UnMarried Wife.

I did not know how I would face the world without him. I was where I was that day because of him. Thoughts started flying in my head. If it was education, I was already studying, I had changed jobs and doing a better job, I no longer had thousand friends, I was more like what he had always wanted. All along I had built my entire existence around him. People always said he would leave. I mean, after so many years without popping the question, he is suddenly popping a question to some girl he had just met. He probably did not even know her family yet. He had been part of my family for years. My brothers were like his brothers. My mother took him as her own son. We were family, we are family and now he was bringing another family to disrupt what we had.

I was numb. My whole body was numb. I am a crier, yes, but that day I could not. I could not shed even one drop. I was just numb. I walked out of the car, straight to my room and slept. I could not even dream that night.

I just slept throughout the night feeling absolutely nothing. Everything was numb. I was dead. I was literally dead.

Chapter 11

The Resurrection

They say never write yourself off. There was a point in time when I felt that my life had no meaning. I felt that everything I had worked so hard for all these years had yielded nothing but pain. I had invested every fiber in my body to this. It had appeared to slip right through my figure tips. I was shattered. I was devastated. I was trying to make peace with it. I should have made peace with it. I know I should have but I could not. Instead of being upset and angry at him, I was rather worried about him. Everything he said about her did not seem to fit what he had been working for throughout all his life. Apart from the character he portrayed when he was giving his speak, I sensed no emotions. He was not an emotional person but for him to take such a decision, there should have been some emotions. I felt that it was never about her being the one but rather about him trying to prove a point that he can do it. He was trying to punish me. He had always sad that out of all the pain I had put him through, once he returned the favour, it would be an eternal one. It would be something so simple yet so difficult that I would never recover from it. He was right.

Whatever the outcome of this whole thing, it would always stay with me that he left me, after almost a decade to go and marry someone else. I was never his first choice. I would never be his first choice then because he has done this. I will always be his backup plan just like I had always been. Through everything he had done, he always knew that I would be there waiting for him. Even with this one, he thinks I would still be there waiting for him.

He thought my life would never move on without him on my side. To some extent, he may have been right. There were a lot of things I never had to worry about. He was there.

There were a lot of things he also did not have to worry about, I was there. He was never very close with his mother, but I was. I was the person she would call if she needed something, whether directly from me or from him. She knew I could get to him. I did not mind. I was the wife after all. He also liked it that way. Even after disappearing for months, if asked why, he would say I was there to deal with his family. That was my duty. Maybe I was never his wife but rather his family's wife. In our culture, that accounts for more anyway so it did not bother me. Here we were now. I was not certain what to do. I did not even know whether I was still allowed to talk to his mother. His sister had already distanced herself. She said in not so many words that if his marriage does not work out, it would be my fault. I was pissed at that. These people did not seem to understand their own son. If his marriage was to never workout it would be because of his actions. You can never teach an old dog new tricks.

One sign of disrespect from that wife will be all it would take for him to move on. The sad part would be that he may always be there physically, but he never forgets and never forgives so his heart would no longer be there. I know. I have been picking up the pieces myself for years now. I had made peace that he would never forgive. I had stopped asking for forgiveness. He had always said that people can only ask for forgiveness from God not him. He does not forgive. Sometimes he just let's go. But definitely does not forgive. He also hated people who apologize. He claimed that apologizing is a sign of weakness. A person does something knowing very well how it may turn out. There are always only two possibilities. It would either go according to plan or not. So, a person always knows.

If it does not go according to plan, why waste your breath and apologise then. Just say you did not intend or anticipate that it would turn out that way and move on.

All these things take time to understand. This person has only been with him for few months before they got married.

She clearly did not understand him at all. He was also proud of where he comes from, so he can never really desert his people. The people who made him. The people who gave him that respect he believed he deserves. There were a lot of them. Some, it was because of what he had done for them while others it was about what he had said to them. He had given a lot of youngsters' hope. Some of them are now continuing their studies because of him. Others has also moved on to greater things because of his advises. He was that type of a person, and nothing would ever replace that. Not even an overnight wife.

This is not a movie. This is real life. This is not Las Vegas, no, this is the real world. Something will tick him off and when that happens, that wife would be married to a shell of what she thought she had. He can adopt as many characters as he wants. So, he may be there physically, but definitely he would not care what happens.

I kept contact in with him. It was never about us ever getting back together though but just being friends. He never had and does not have any friends, so I offered myself as a friend. He did not mind. So, we kept in contact. I had not gotten around stopping calling him love or babe, or all those words. He mentioned once that I should remember that I am just his ex and should not be using such terms. To me, it did not matter. I used them anyway. If they pissed him off that much, then I would know. For the years I had been with him, I had learned a few things or two about him so I would know if he really did not like me calling him those names.

Our conversations were just fun and jokes. We spoke about how his marriage was, his life, etc. It was all fun and games. He always painted this perfect marriage picture since day one. But I could sense it. It was never that rosy. First, the wife had a different background from him so he could never accept some of the things she believed in. I had come to learn that she was an "all bubbly person" with a lot of friends. He would never accept that. He could not for years with me, he would not start now. She was from an advantaged background and a part of him had certain reservations about such.

To him, people who grew up in an advantaged environment have no excuse not to have a good life. They should have gone to the best schools and at age 26, they should be having a life of their own. I had come to learn that she was still a part-time first year student; she did not have a stable job and had no prospects of ever being at his level. He could never stand that. He had always wanted a wife more powerful than him. That is why I was never his first choice. To him, he had always said that "if she earns more than me and she is more powerful than me but yet still with me, then she's there for me, for who I am and not what I am". This woman was nothing like that. Maybe he had seen something special about her, but she was not getting anywhere close to what he had hoped she was or would become. This marriage was doomed even before we even started talking again. So, if it does not work out, it can never be blamed on me. I was just an ex willing to be a friend and I must admit, I was hoping to be a friend with benefits. Until this day, I could still do anything to be his friend with benefits.

I would not say that I was the best in the world, but I can pat myself at the back that I offered him everything he needed. He was never a classic person. I think the watching of porn messed up his head. But well, maybe it just woken up an animal in him. I know for sure there are very few women out there who would ever keep up.

Although I was certain he could never have had anything close to what we had with anyone else, I would randomly ask him directly.

Not for the answer he would give because I already knew it, but for assurity that I was indeed the best he had ever had. She was an almost plus size. A size on the upper side of my size I should put it, so I know that she was not really his ideal. He had certain fantasies that only a particular size would be able to fulfil. So once again, it would not have been me. I would not have been the reason if anything was to happen if his marriage never works out. There was just a lot that was anti-him.

Although he liked me in a certain size, he had always mentioned that it would not hurt to gain one or two pounds. As the age was going, the exercises were not that often, I was starting to gain some pounds. I still maintained the size but on the upper limit of it. I used to tease him that maybe it was because I was tiny that is why he left but at least then I had gained. He called it "firm" not gaining. I would agree with him. Gaining would mean I would change a size, but I did not, it was just that my clothes fitted me differently. Those were the things we spoke about. We were like friends. Something we had never been for all these years. The problem with this was that as friend, we could tell things about each other that we could not while we were together. He knew I was seeing someone. He knew I was sleeping with that someone. Well, he could not say anything because he was permanently sleeping with someone too. At some point he did claim not to, but this was me, I knew when he was lying. He was lying. The sad part on my side was that everything I did never mattered.

It was like I had become him in his past life. I would be with someone for a moment and turn out to hate them the next moment.

Fortunately, I had always committed to him. So, I could not sleep around. I just could not bear the thought of another man seeing me naked. Although John thought I was, I was actually not.

I knew him too well. I knew him well enough to know that even if he was getting it every night, he could never be satisfied with the same offering all the time. Even while he used to deny these things when he was with me, he used to say, "whoever eats the same dinner every night for the whole year?". It was humanly impossible. If they did, they probably had reached the misserability level that is beyond comprehension. I therefore knew one thing. As he had said it himself on a number of occasions, I had saved him from a lot of things. I had saved him from going around getting every skanky he could get his hands on. I was that "sure-case" as he would put it to his colleagues. I was always there. He could wake up at midnight and come to my house just for one thing and he knew I would be there.

This time it was no different. If I had any hope of what may happen in the far future, I had to emotionally avail myself to him. Whether he wanted me or not, it did not matter. What mattered was that he needed to know that if he ever feels that the same super is not working out for him, he could always be served a different one without any hustle, irrespective of everything that had happened. It would have not been a difficult thing for him.

I know he can put his feelings on the side when it comes to certain things. He could just do the same now. I was rather "it's rather me than someone else". He would be safe that way. I would be safe too. His wife would be safe as well because the last thing I would ever want to hear was that he was sick or dead or something. I would not be able to live with myself if that was to ever happen.

It was not like he would be trying to ask me to kill someone, he would be just getting what had always belonged, belongs and would always belong to him ever since that pact I made. It was a pact that can never be reversed unfortunately. Only he can release me. Even if I wanted to, it would be all a mess. He is the only one who can allow it to happen. Even with that, all he would have to do is to open his heart to it, and then I would be free. I would be free to start a real relationship with anyone. But till then, I am stuck. I am stuck in this relationship that does not even exist. I am just the other person, and he knows it too and I think he is capitalizing on it. He knows I have nowhere to go. I can go nowhere without his approval.

I never understood why he kept me while he was carrying on with his life. Not that I had a problem with it, but I would have wished he could let me go.

Looking back now, I am glad he never did. Maybe if he had done so, I would not be here today. I would have slipped back to my old self. I would have probably been even a worse mess than I was before him. I am glad he never did. For many years, I was the one who saved him, now he was the one who saved me.

I will forever be grateful for that. I would do anything to show him that even if he were to disappear for a century, I would still be waiting when he returned. Even if he were never to return, I would still be available when he visited. I would welcome him with open arms. I hold no grudge against him. I could not. How could a wife hold a grudge against her husband for making an impulsive decision that was pushed by her? It would never make sense. Besides all that, I made a commitment. The commitment was not to him or for him; it was a commitment between me and myself.

I would always be by his side. I would always be his wife. I am his wife, and he is my husband. Only that.

I am his UnMarried Wife.

Chapter 12

The Now

Many years had passed. He was still with his wife. He was getting more miserable as time went by. I did not know how bad it actually was. All he ever said was "All I ever wanted was RESPECT". I did not know how bad the situation was. I had always known that he never appreciated people who disrespected him. Although he preferred individual thinkers and hated submissive people, he always made it a point that if you argue with him, please argue with dignity. Have some respect, your point will still be heard.

With women, he had a much-defined type that he believed would be the one to keep him or tame him as he would put it. "A woman must learn only two things, RESEPCT and HUMILITY. They must either not be so smart and submissive or very smart and dominant. In the latter case, I would trust their judgement, or they would accept my judgement. Anything in between is trouble. Imagine a not so smart person who cannot be submissive or a very smart one who is overly submissive, that relationship would never work. If she is too smart but overly submissive, she would go with whatever I say, and we would lose out on her bright ideas.

If she is not so smart but yet not submission, she would be arguing all my points without seeing the big picture. That what no so smart people do if they cannot accept that the other person must take control". That was exactly how he would put it.

Such statements are the reasons why I had always allowed him to lead. There would be things I would not bother about even learning. Sometimes it would be something as simple as new technology. I knew he was there. That was his place. I would suggest but never advise on serious issues. I would live them for him to make the decisions.

What I knew was that whatever decision he made; it would be the best decision for the situation at hand. He was a focused person; he was very protective of his image. He was a proud person and very thorough when it comes to how he is perceived, so every decision he would ever make would revolve around that. He could never let me down. I know you might be thinking that, but he did let me down. He left and went and married a stranger. Well, here's a thing. He was my daughter's father for years knowing very well who the biological father was. He knew that everyone understood the situation. He had introduced us to his family and had explained the situation to them. He had defended his decision to be with me for years. My family knew that he knew the real story behind my daughter's biological father matter.

Yes, he did, for years knew all this, defended all this, had to write off certain people in his life who had an issue with all this, until that day.

That day when he found out that everything, he thought he knew was all a lie. The father he was told was the one was actually not. The fact that I was still in contact with my daughter's biological father also hurt him. The fact that my family knew that he knew the real story was all a lie. I had lied to them. I had told them I had told him the truth. He even had some of my aunties asking him when he would be paying damages for his daughter. The story he had given to his family was all a lie. I had forced him to lie.

If the truth was to come out, he would be looked at as someone who had been duped into a relationship based on lies. That will be like slicing through his soul with a sharp sword. He is perceived as a well calculating and smart person. He could not have been used like this for this long. So, all this shattered him. The only revenge tactic that he thought off was leaving. Meeting someone and getting married. He knew how much I wanted to get married but after the real truth surfaced, he realized that maybe all these years were just wasted years.

Maybe he should have left me long ago. Unfortunately for me, while he was reeling from this pain, someone came into his life. Everything changed. Life started to make a different sense to him. He moved on. Got married and had kids.

Now we are here. He is still married because apparently, he cannot get divorced. He can never allow his only blood child to be raised by another man. He had always had a problem with having his own kids because of his experiences as a child. He could not allow his blood child to go through that.

That is why he kept in contact with my daughter even when he left. He was still the only father she had chosen to accept. He loved happy kids. So, he could not leave just because the wife did not turn out to what he had hoped for. He had to stay.

He was burning inside. He could not even come to see me just for that destress laugh. His wife would never allow him to come to my hometown alone. She knew my existence and she knew that there was a very high likelihood that if he were to come, obviously he would come and see his daughter, I would be there and probably we would end up in some shady hotel somewhere for the night. She could not contemplate that. She never allowed him that chance. She thought she was doing her family a favour. She thought the more he saw me, the more he would think maybe he shouldn't have left.

That is where her first mistake was. I was never the problem; I was the solution to their marriage. If he had kept seeing me, he could not even think of leaving her because he thought she would think it was because of me. Without me in the picture, he could leave. Hard to explain, but I was one of the reasons he could never leave. She still could not allow him to go home on his own, just because his hometown was just around the corner from my hometown.

That was it. That was her biggest mistake. All those stunts made John feel controlled.

Now you cannot cage a lion forever. It ate him alive. The wife was close to her family and friends. She would see them as and when she felt like it. He never objected.

He was always the type who hated controlling and despised being controlled. All his family and people who may be considered as friends were all around my hometown so because he could not come to it, it meant that he could not see them as often as he would have wanted. That is not what you do to a man like him. He may have not been a buddy buddy family man type, but he always wanted to see that everyone was fine. If he could not see them, then he would not know if they were really fine or not.

Months went by, years went by. Family members passed on, former colleagues got married, divorced, got promotions, got new jobs, died, had kids, retired, family members even changed their surnames, had functions, parties, funerals, weddings, etc. He was never there. I guess the wife was happy that he had cut ties with his birthplace. I am sure she thought that as years went by, he would accept that he had a new life that did not involve anyone from his past. All this, it was just to spite me and my daughter. It was never about him or her, but just to spite me.

For what? because she had found emails between myself and John many years ago when I used to still call him love and babe or one of those sweet words love birds call each other. She thought that isolating him would take him. At the same time, as time went by, my biggest concern was how he was feeling because I knew that either way, whether it was me or someone else, he would still look for a comfort zone.

Every man or woman always look for a comfort place. He may end up with someone somewhere who would not care for his family or his wife. At least I did. If there is one thing I never wanted, it was for them to ever separate because of me or something I had done. However, I could not refuse helping him whenever and wherever I could. He was still my man after all, just married to someone else.

He had an image to maintain so he could not go around sleeping with strangers. He was not the type who enjoyed being known. These days, the world is very small. The last thing he would have wanted was to bump into a crazy booty call at the mall while he was with his family. With me, he knew I would never do anything. I could even pretend as if I do not know him. We had done that for years while we were together. We would have the craziest night the previous day and pretend as if we did not know each other the following day. He knew I could do that. I think his wife also did. But it did not matter anymore.

I had not heard from him for many years. I had not even seen him for many years. Because of all this, I had missed his grandmother's funeral and even his mother's funeral. His mother had been like my second mother for years so it broke me that I could not even be there because everybody knew me, and I was avoiding all the drama. I had come to learn how dramatic his wife is, so I decided not to.

My daughter was old enough now. She had completed University and working as a Doctor at a local hospital.

I had grown up too. I had left my normal corporate work and focused on my gift and business. The gift I had always suppressed because I wanted to live what people would consider as a normal life. I had moved out of my mother's house and was now staying with some of my family members as I could not stay alone, and I could no longer allow the house I had built to stand by itself. Besides, I could not deal with my gift under my mother's roof.

I was still there. I was still emotionally there for him

without him knowing. I was always praying for him. I was praying that someday he finds what he was looking for even if that was not me. I knew he was not happy, but work and school kept him sane.

But years were going. Interest in his work was fading. School passion was also fading. He had nothing much to keep him sane. His kids were grownups now.

They were starting to leave their own lives. He had nothing to hang on to but the hope that someday things will be fine. That is what he always told himself. To me, he was still "my-everything".

He was still my husband, and I was still his UnMarried Wife.

One Saturday morning my phone rang. I picked it up. It was his sister. The very same one who distanced herself from me believing that I was the reason why John's marriage was not going well. I answered. It was a very brief call. He was gone. He was finally gone. John was gone. He had woken up one morning, went to work, cleared out his office, printed out all his life insurance and funeral covers paperwork, left his work laptop in his office drove home, put the papers on the countertop and drove off.

Few minutes later the wife received a call from the vehicle tracking company. They had received a collision alarm from John's vehicle and his phone was dead. They told her where it happened. It was just 2.5km from his house. Eyewitnesses say they saw everything. His car came and stopped at a stop street as per the road traffic rules. A truck came on the other side. It waited for him go through but he flagged it to proceed as if his car had stalled. As the truck was halfway into the junction, all they had was a big bang. He had accelerated into the truck. He was dead. John was dead. He had committed suicide by collision. It had always been his crazy fantasy that he would die on a car crash. He had always seemed to know how it would happen. But the truck had never been part of the plan. John had taken his life. He was no more. His sister hung up without even giving me the details of the funeral. I wanted to be there. I wanted to see him one last time, but I could not. Not like this. I did not want to cause any drama.

Once again, the lies started. I had to come up with a comfortable lie why her father had died.

I told my daughter that he had had an accident. A truck had failed to stop on the stop sign and drove over him. The tracking company still had my email as a back-up email on the system, so the driving history was also forwarded to me. It showed that at the time of the collision, he was driving at just under 20km/h. It showed that he had stopped at the stop sign and upon driving through, the accident happed. So, it made sense to everyone that it was the truck that had failed to stop. Unfortunately, the truck had no records. No one even believed the eyewitnesses or the truck driver. Her father was gone. I claimed that I could not tell her earlier because I did not want to affect her international stay. When all this happened, she was away on an international business or training of some sort.

All we could ever do was to go to his grave afterwards to pay our last respect. And that is exactly what we did. The question that always lingered was, "why he never left if it was so difficult?". One part of me was upset with this but another part also understood. John had made a commitment. He had done a similar thing with me in the past. With all the allegations and problems, we had gone through, he had all the time and chance in the world to leave but he did not. He hung by until that stupid day. He could not have left his new family no matter what the situation was. He hung by until that stupid day when he decided to take his own life. That how broken my John was.

Here I was.

I still believed that he was my husband, and I was his wife. Yes, I was still his UnMarried Wife, yet I could not help him see a reason to live any longer, to live to see his grand kids. I was hopeless. I was shattered. I felt the world closing in on me. I had no more strength to fight. I was feeling weak. I felt cold. All this long I was wondering in the wilderness of thoughts. Everything was getting blurry. I heard siren sounds, announcement sounds and a lot of noise but from the distance. It got darker and darker, colder and colder. I was out. I passed out again. I was gone.

Chapter 13

It Was Just a Dream

I opened my eyes. Everything was white. The room I was in was painted white. The bed sheets were all white. My mind started recouping itself. I woke up. I was in hospital. My daughter was the only one in the room. She looked tired. She was sleeping on the couch next to my bed. I let her be. I could not recall what had happened. I tried to recall my day or what day that was. The last I remembered was the phone call. I remember the phone call. I could not remember what it was all about, but I remember it had something to do with John. I had a headache. I had a terrible headache. It reminded me of all the headaches John had complained about many years ago. I looked around. There was a jug of water. I took it. As I was trying to lift it up, my hand shook, and the jug dropped. The noise of the class breaking woke my daughter up. She smiled and held my hand "Mama, mama, you awake?". She said seeming happy. "Don't worry I will explain everything when we get home. The Doctor checked and there is nothing wrong. They were just waiting for you to wake up then they would let us go".

I woke up; I was still dressed up in my clothes. So, we signed some few papers. The nurse said, "Well, you have a smart daughter here. She will explain everything to you. Now go have some rest. Take it easy ok.". We left the hospital.

As we arrived home, my mind was starting to come back. I think I know what had happened. Before I could even start recalling, I fell asleep. Again, I was asleep.

I did not dream of anything that day. I was just flat out. I think it might have been the medication they gave me at the hospital.

It was a lovely day. The summer breeze was abuzz. The birds were singing, the trees were hissing from the breeze cutting through them. The dogs outside were barking, the neighbour's cat was screaming. The Television was turned on but the volume so soft I could not hear it. I would not hear it even when I walked into the kitchen. The kitchen had a serving opening into the sitting room so from anywhere in the kitchen, one could see the entire sitting room. I could see the television was on but there was no one in front of it. The house was quiet. It actually felt like a deserted house. The dishes in the kitchen were inside the sink filled with soap water as if someone had tried to wash them but just left. The television was on. The microwave was making that noise as if someone had just completed heating up something. Everyday life was in motion, but the house was deserted. The front door was closed. I thought it was locked.

The kitchen door was definitely locked as it was the first thing I tried to open when I got into the kitchen. I always preferred the door opened every time I was working in the kitchen.

I was not there to do work that day though; I was there to get something to drink. I was thirsty. It had been a long day that felt like a very long time. My head was trying to process everything that has happened.

Now I remembered. It was that phone call from John's sister that started everything. My heart was beating fast again. I started having mini-panic attacks. I could not breathe. As I limped into the seating room, my daughter walked in from the main door. She had a doggy bowl with her. She seemed as if she had been feeding the dogs outside.

"What the hell is happened here?" I heard myself asking. My daughter has returned home. When did she return from the overseas trip? And why? Thousand questions were filling up my space. The breathing had subsided. I was still in shock.

"Hi mommy, are you ok?" my daughter asked. I just sat there and looked at her. Just yesterday she was a child. Now she was all grown up. Life is full of surprises neh.

"The doctor said you must take your medication every time your heart starts beating faster", she said. Once again, I was just staring at her.

"You had a panic attack yesterday and we had to take to the hospital", she proceeded.

"For what?", I asked.

"You were out, completely out. It was like someone choke-slammed you in a wrestling match. You couldn't breather", she said with a smack as if this was all a joke. "But you will be fine".

After I had taken my medication, the memories from the day before started coming back. My memory started coming back. "It was today. It was just a day after yesterday. My daughter did not go to school today because there was no one to stay home with me for today. My mother had gone to work. My brothers and sister had also gone to work", speaking to myself.

I was a couple of years younger. My daughter was still in high school. My mind was all over the show. I was trying to recall each and every detail of the day before.

The phone call. Yes, that what started everything. I received a call. It had something to do with John. I cannot remember the details, but it had something to do with his death. I picked up my phone, looked at received calls. There was nothing about John's sister. She had not called. Instead, there was a call from John himself. How could this be? Was it before he committed suicide or was, I just dreaming? I redialed the number. John picked up.

I froze. I did not know why I froze. Maybe it was the coldness in his voice, maybe it was how quickly he picked or maybe it was the fact that he picked up at all.

"Hi, how are you", I asked trying to compose myself.

"Well, I guess I should say I'm fine or better, I'm breathing", he responded.

It was him. The voice was his. So, it must have been him. "Well, I was just checking up on you", I said.

"Okay sharp", he responded.

I could tell he was in no mood to talk so I hung up. While seating there, the television was on the news channel, so they had time and date on the screen. I looked at it, it did not make sense. Was I dreaming? This was over 2 decades ago. I min, if the date and time on the television screen were real, why were they replaying such old news? As I was busy trying to figure things out, my daughter came in. She asked me if I was fine to know the details of what had happened. I was ready. I wanted this whole thing to go away. I wanted to know what was happening. Was I dreaming or had I been dreaming all along? I was confused.

"Well, I don't know what happened before we got to you but on arrival, the phone was still on, and Daddy was on the other side. We didn't want to worry him since he is far, we just told him that you slipped and sprained your ankle and dropped the phone so we will call when you are fine. The truth is you were out. Somehow you collapse. We tried everything but it did not work. We couldn't wait for the ambulance, so my uncle took you to hospital. In there, you were just out. At some point the Doctors thought you were dead because you were not breathing but everything else seemed fine, so they just let you lie there.

I stayed behind in case you woke up and as you would remember, I was woken up by you breaking the glass".

That was it. My daughter told me the doctors said it must have been stress or something, but I would be fine.

Now everything was coming back. It had only been three years since John had left. My daughter was still in high school. I was still at home. My mother was still alive. John was still alive. Everything that had happened had happened in my sleep. I was dreaming. Or maybe I should say, I had a premonition on how things would turn out. I had always known John as a strong person.

The thought of him ever committing suicide was just not adding up. For years he had said that he would die on a vehicle accident but not just any vehicle, a very powerful vehicle. He was still driving an ordinary car so he could not die now. He is not even dead.

It all donned on me. The phone call, now I remembered. I was telling him that I was pregnant. The excitement came back again. "Damn I am pregnant", I accidentally said it loud. Before I could retract it, my daughter was all excited about it and she started her own dream here. She was all about how she will help her sister with school homework just like daddy has done for her. They would go to the mall every weekend to play games. By the time she would be in high school, she would have graduated as a doctor and would take her sister in as special nurse in her surgery. She was on and on and on about this coming sister.

"Who said she's your sister not your brother?", I asked.

"I know cos daddy loves girls", she responded.

Well, she was right about one thing. Daddy did love girls. I mean he did prefer girls over boys.

And yes, he did love girls so either way, she was right, daddy do love girls.

All along, I had been dreaming. I think it might have been the conversation I had with John. Here I was, my first daughter did not know her biological father. He was hidden from her. It was said it was meant to protect her. Because of that secret, the only father she had always known had left. He had gone on to get married and had two other kids who had never met their older sister, my first born. Now I was pregnant. I was pregnant with a child that will never know her biological father either. The problem this time around though would be who would be her father figure. Some people would think the reason she does not have a father is because her mother had slept with a married man. A married ex. Some would believe my story that I had gone into the sperm bank and got an anonymous donor so I could never know who the biological father is.

If John decided to pretend as if he was the father, then it would actually validate his wife's allegations that he was cheating with me. This was an unwinnable case. Either way, when it comes up that I'm pregnant, everyone would think its John's child. Whether it is John's or not is immaterial. People will believe whatever they want to believe.

Instead of dwelling on my dream, I was now happy with the news I just remembered. Here I was. I was pregnant. I was finally pregnant. I had always wanted a child with John. He never wanted a child.

For some time, I actually believed him until he told me that he had just had a child. Throughout his wife's pregnancy, he never mentioned anything until the child was about two months old.

This told me that maybe it was not that John did not want a child, but he just did not want one with me. But here I was now. I was pregnant with my second and last born. It's a girl. I was ecstatic. I wondered how John would treat her. Would he take her as his child and treat her like all his other kids or would she be different? Different is a sense that those who would believe she is his daughter would think he treats her one way or the other because she was a love child and those who would not believe that she was his child would think it was because maybe John is still doing what he had done all along, protecting my image and his too.

It mattered not anymore, nothing mattered anymore. John can move on with his life as he had decided but now at least I know we will always share a special bond. He will always be my husband and I will always be his Unmarried Wife. Now I am not just his UnMarried Wife but also a mother of his lovely daughters too.

Chapter 14

The Epilogue

John was still married to his wife.

I had given birth to a lovely, beautiful daughter.

I named her Pearl. I, myself had been called "The Precious Pearl" by some anyway. This was not the name John had always given to his non-existent daughter, but it would do since it was a name, he had used quiet often. This was my way of keeping that bond I had always wanted with John.

John was content with the presence of Pearl. He loved her like any of his other kids, both biological and non-biological kids.

People were talking behind my back that I had repeated what I had done before, claiming that John was the father of my second child which actually was my 3rd child.

It was not the same though. This time around, John and I knew the truth.

Some family members too knew the truth, but it was decided that things would be whatever anyone said. John and I were too old to defend nonsense. We were content with our separate lives.

John's wife though was not very impressed. She was happy that it was said that I had a child, and she was certain it was not John's.

Unfortunately, she was later told that John was the Godfather. Now she was not sure. A part of her always told her that John was still seeing me.

Then that very same part was trying to convince her that the child was actually John's. Unfortunately, she would never know the truth. No one will. John and I had decided that it was better that way. We were tired of explaining things that did not need any explanation to people whom some did not even matter. All that mattered to us was that every child should be given a chance to live a decent life. That is what we were only concerned about.

The strangest thing though was that out of everything that had happened between John and I or John and his wife, there has always been a child that had never came up in any of the conversations. That was my child fathered by John just a year after he had gotten married to his wife. Because I did not want to cause any trouble in John's marriage, we had decided that the child would be raised by my sister, as her own.

It did not matter or make any difference to me because we were all staying under the same roof anyway.

So technically, John had three biological daughters and two non-biological ones. It was a squad of girls.

People never knew this though. Even some of our family members did not understand our setup. That was how we preferred our lives to be. We were better off apart than together. In that case, John could carry on living his double or triple or multi-life. That was what he had done for years in any case. Even during his childhood, he would change characters just to survive. People who knew him from school or the streets never knew how bad things were at home. People who knew him from the city never knew how good life was at school. People who knew him from his neighbourhood always wondered how he survived. He had always been a strange character. Until this day, he had never had friends, which should give you a hint on what type of a person he was. He had perfected character multiplicity in anyway, so I was fine with that.

John himself was no different. He was not getting any better. He was forever stressed, and he had thought that the presence of Pearl would change things. He had though that I would move on with my then new life and his wife would trust him again. However, it was never to be. Instead, it got even worse at his home.

He could no longer take all what he perceived as emotional abuse from a woman who had brought him nothing but misery in life.

A part of him wished for people to believe that Pearl was his biological daughter but then another part wished that people would never know if she was his biological daughter or not. In that case, those who thought he was a perfect husband would see that it was not a case while those who thought he was not a good father would see that he actually took care of all his children.

He had always hoped that his wife would wake up one day, pack her bags and leave. At least if that had happened, he would hurt only for a while but would get over it. Without it happening, the pain from his emotional abuse would never end. He sometimes believed that the only way to end the pain would be to end it forever. That would have been to take his own life. It was a selfish thought but sometimes it becomes the only choice.

For me, I was happy that John was alive. I was happy that my kids would grow up knowing that their father loved them too although he was not around. I was happy with my decision. I had made a commitment to myself. I had accepted him with all his flaws and had fought tooth and nail to stay with him. I was not going to stop then.

Ow, by the way I am actually married now. No, not to John, but to this loving gentleman I met a few years after John left.

THE U̶N̶MARRIED WIFE

I was and will always be his Wife, his UnMarried Wife.

The Unmarried Wife
By
Aliana Marshall

Copyright © 2019 by Aliana Marshall

Chapter 15

The Preview

Life is a journey, not a destination. Life evolves and no one can ever tell what tomorrow would look like. Everything that we do or say had already been said or done for us by our guardian angels. All we ever actually do is to execute their plan. We do that from the day we are born until the day we die. Afterwards, we take a different form of life. It is only during that period that we may claim to have control over our lives. Unfortunately, that period only comes after our physical existence in this world has ended. It only comes at a period whereby we can no longer act on anything that relates to our living lives in this world. Some philosophers would tell you that, "the only thing you can do in that afterlife state is to fulfil your duties by guiding those who are still breathing the earthly breath".

Writing has a definite start but there is no definite end. A writer decides to pause their story at any point in time. It can be thus said that writing is a journey, not a destination. Every story only has a definable definite start, but none has a definite end.

……………Every story evolves………………

This chapter is my introduction to another life, a different story, a story about a man and a woman who got married believing that it was the right thing to do. However, as it turned out, it was the worst thing they could have ever done to themselves. Everything started falling apart, especially for Adolph. His guardian angels had left him.

Prior to everything, Adolph had lived a particular life for almost three decades of his existence. He had defied the norm. He was abnormally-normal. He was content with that. His guardian angels had been with him through thick and thin. He sure had a lot of things. His guardian angels had guided him from the extreme poverty he grew up into the life he was then living.

He was one of those people that people close to him kept wondering how he did it. It was no miracle. He was a hard worker. He was a focused person. He spent most of his time focusing on the positivities of life instead of all the hardships he was going through. He had worked harder than anyone I know. He had made it. He was living an acceptable life according to his standards. He had never been one to care much about relationships. He had claimed that love is not for everyone but for those who believe in it, yet he never really explained whether he, himself believed in it or not.

That was his life. Until that one day. Until the day he suddenly decided to be normal.

He considered it the biggest test his guardian angels had ever given him. He felt that his guardian angels were testing his happiness with his life. But, no, the test became his new life. He was then normal. He was doing things normal people did. He was going to church more often, he was married, he had a family, and he was just a normal person. It was that change that made him believe that his guardian angels had turned their back on him. Everything; from finances, birth family relationships, career, social and even his self-confidence had subsided.

He was just a shell of his former self. To him, all that were the results of the decision he had made. The decision to live a normal life was his biggest miscalculation.

He felt that his guardian angels were upset with him that after all those years, after everything they had guided him through, after all the effort they had put in for him to accept who he was the way he was, boom, he woke up and wanted to be normal. Sometimes he felt that maybe they were not equipped to guide a normal person. "Maybe that is the problem", he would say.

He was married. His wife was miserable, he was miserable. He would be away from home on unnecessary work trips just to avoid being at home. The kids did not help much. The arrival of a second child could not help either. He was just a miserable man in a marriage from hell. That is why I had titled my next book.

The Marriage from Hell"

..............Here is the preview..............

"One person's blessing may be the next person's curse". That is what philosophers say.

I am no philosopher. I am not even going to claim to be one. To me, a blessing is a blessing. The phrase "blessing" is contextual as it is. Sometimes one may think that something is a blessing only to realize many years later that it was actually not a blessing. They say a marriage is a blessing. Some people would do anything to get married. Some people think getting married is an achievement. Well, it can be classified as a blessing depending on which side of the fence they are standing on.

To me, the way I look at life, marriage is a process of getting one person to remove themselves from who they were and adopt a character either called a wife or a husband.

...................The Beginning......................

It was a sunny day. The birds were singing. The trees were swaying from side to side. It was not windy but just breezy. In the coast, they would call it a sea breeze. That was what it felt like. The trucks were hauling the produce in and out. Some truck drivers were shouting for others to move, and others were shouting for some to give them a break. Chris was shouting in his French voice something to Sakasee.

If you did not understand French, you would not understand what was being said. Mashaba was busy sweeping a clean floor. Yes, he pretended as if he was busy by sweeping and already clean floor. Lollipop was staring at her phone as if she was waiting for an e-wallet. Even if she was, what was she going to do with it because she was in the bushes there? That place was far from anything. It was a place where even public taxi business did not see any potential for getting into business there. People took lifts to get to work.

It was time to change shifts. That would be just before 2pm. People were coming in in drips and draps. The morning shift was preparing to go home. They were woke. They were the most energetic beings in the entire factory. People were always like that, when it was about time to go home, they would always become the happiest and liveliest beings in this world. This was in exception, off course, for those who did not look forward to going home.

At the back, the water pumps were running. The water level alarm was on. The water level had dropped. This was the only water that the factory used. The factory was supplied with water from the river nearby. The water would be cleaned and purified through a number of filtration processes which included sand filters, cloth filters and reverse osmosis filters. This was the water that people drank in the factory.

The day was sunny. The water was a must. That place could get hot sometimes. It would get close to 45 degrees Celsius sometimes.

If the water level alarm was on, it meant that the pumps were not running, the filterers were blocked or the water flow from the river was inadequate.

That day, it was not the filters; it was not the pumps, so it must have been the water flow from the river. Adolph sent Tibos to the river to check. First, he had to open all the filters at the factory pump house, clean them, put them back, reset the alarm and wait to see what happened. If the alarm came back, he would have to switch off the system and go down to the river.

As expected, the alarm could not be reset, so Tibos had to go to the river. He took his tool bag, asked one of the assistants to go with him.

He could walk, but it was far, and the weather was not helping. To get to the river, you needed to drive through a drive section that was well known for its presence of dangerous snakes. That was a desert. The factory and the river were located in one of the driest and hottest states in the country. The state also became the country's coldest state during the winter season. Tibos had to use the company vehicle to get to the river where the first pump house was located.

He went to where the vehicle keys were normally kept. He could not find them. He had to go to the office block and ask around as to who may had used the vehicle last because the vehicle itself was parked outside the office block.

After going up and down, talking to different individuals, finally the vehicle keys were found. Tibos took his tools and drove to the river.

Before you get to the river, there was a gate that was meant to keep people away from the company property. People used to use the gate when they were going fishing. Fishing was not allowed in that river, but people still did it anyway. No one from the company could stop them. No one actually bothered. Sometimes employees used to ask the fishermen for some of the fish they caught. Sometimes the fishermen used to catch the fish, take it home, cook it and bring some the following day for some of the employees. I think it was their way of bribing them so they could carry on fishing without anyone from the company harassing them. They were trying to put food on the table like all these people hovering around with blue and while overalls.

The blue overalls were for the people working on the biscuit sections and the white overalls were for the people who were working on flour section. The company produced biscuits from the flour it had produced. Some of the produced flour was sold in bulk. These were the trucks that were coming in and going out that day.

They were taking the bulk flour to bakeries and supermarkets.

Although pedestrians could jump over the gate leading to the river, a vehicle could not, so someone had to open the gate for the vehicle to drive through. Tibos drove and stopped in from of the gate. He asked Sakasee to go and open the gate. Sakasee refused. He said he had once seen a very big snake there, so he was scared. They had a small argument about it until Tibos went and opened the gate himself.

At the river, the water pipe sucking the water from the river to the sand filters at the pump station was blocked. Tibos and Sakasee cleared the blockage and drove off back to the factory.

At the factory they went and checked the factory pump house. The water level alarm was still on but at least the flow was then better than before. They left the alarm on and were going to go back after an hour to check. It should be fine by then. The water levels should rise. When it rose to 70%, the level alarm would stop.

Back inside, Lollipop was still on her phone. She was always a trouble that one. Apart from such things as being on the phone all the time, she also left her workstation more often than necessary. Operators were allowed to leave work their stations. They would leave their workstations to go and freshen up or for lunch. But with Lolli, it was different. She would leave her working station almost every twenty minutes. She had a smoking addiction. She smoked like there was no tomorrow.

Lolli was his crush. Lolli was Adolph's crush. Well, maybe not a crush as such because everyone knew, and he made it known. They were never together though. She was this young beautifully quiet girl. She looked much younger than her age. She was different from the rest. A lot of the other girls liked Adolph too.

Most of them liked him because, first, he was not from around the neighbourhood, secondly, to them; he was their ticket out or up the corporate ladder. He was a manager. Girls liked managers in that neighbourhood.

If you went out with a manager, you were most likely to get a promotion. That is how they looked at it. So, they had their eyes on Adolph.

On the other side, there was this one girl who did not even standout. Some of the other girls did not like her.

They would complain that she smoked too much, and she carried herself like a guy. Strangely enough though, all the difference is what Adolph liked about her. He was a very particular person. From the posture, the looks, the walk, the size, he was very particular when it came to his women. Lollipop was different. She walked slightly like a guy. Not really like a guy but surely, she did not have a catwalk walk. She never dressed up in skirts. She was a typical Tomboy. She even played soccer and she spoke the guy's lingo. She was someone you would never imagine Adolph falling for. But, alas, here they were, he could do anything to get her but one thing he could never do was to use his position because to him that has always been a tactical statutory rape. He could never contemplate that. So, he tried the best way he knew how. He was a charming guy.

When Tibos came back from the water reservoir at the back, he did not go to the office or the workshop. He went to the operations side. He was then standing there with Lolli. Lolli had put her phone in the pocket by then and was focusing on her job. Tibos, as usual, was making small talks with the ladies on the line.

This was an environment where majority of people were at an entry level, and a very few were earning above poverty line salaries. People like Tibos were like small celebrities. The ladies loved them. They loved them because on weekends they would go to the township and spend time and money with these ladies.

Throughout all this, Adolph was nowhere to be seen. Right then he would be somewhere in the mix there. He would probably be somewhere close to Lolli. They enjoyed talking to each other. Lolli knew no one would complain that she was not working while she was talking to him, and Adolph knew no one would ever question him.

He was the one person who kept the machinery going. No one understood what he was doing and how he was doing it. All they knew was that if a machine stops, he would be there to fix it.

That day though, he was nowhere to be seen. He had been looking for houses on the internet. He was actually looking for his first house. It would be one of his highest achievements if he got one. He had spoken to his bank, and he knew how much he qualified for. He was busy on the internet. He had identified some houses very far from the place he was working in. He, however, had a plan. His plan was to get the house and rent it out while he was looking for work in the area where the house would be located.

He made a first call to some guy. They spoke and things did not work out.

The second call he made would be the call that changed his life forever. She sounded smart. I guess she knew her job. Either way, she sounded smart. She was a working woman who sounded smart. Everyone knew the property business was not a very easy industry to work in. So, if she sounded that smart and worked in the property industry, she must have been worth his attention. That was the woman he spoke to on the second call.

After all the details he needed from her, he put down the phone. Tibos had entered the office while he was still on the phone. As soon as he put down the phone, he told

Tibos that he had just found a wife. Yes, a wife. This person who never wanted to get married or have kids was suddenly saying he had found a wife. She must have been special.

Tibos wondered what that woman had said to convince this hard-core manager that she was going to be his wife. But that was it, Adolph was hooked. He was going to make sure he meets that lady. It did not matter that she was far.

She was so far that even with Adolph's driving skills and his super-fast car, it would take him six hours to get there.

It was going to happen, one way of the other. And happen it did.

After that phone call, he called again and arranged to come and view one of the houses. As the Agent is supposed to, she asked some questions which included a question about who was going to stay in the house because Adolph was far. Adolph told her she would stay in it. It was all roses.

That very same weekend Adolph drove to see the house. It was not about the house, but about putting the face to the voice and kindness.

Life works in mysterious ways. That day they ended up driving around for six hours looking at only four houses. They spoke a lot though. She told him she had a child. She actually said she was married. He jokingly said she needed to do something about that. She needed to correct that mistake.

Although Adolph would never go for married women, the way the conversation was going, it sounded like just an excuse. There was nothing tangible about the marriage. She had a ring, yes, but Adolph had a ring too. He had had it for over a year by that time so he knew that a ring may mean absolutely nothing. It may just be there for decoration.

She was everything he wished she could be. She was

good looking, well-built and well postured, she sounded smart, she sounded strong, hardworking and a focused person. He liked that. He was sure she was the one. He had just found himself a wife here.

That evening while driving back to his place, he could not stop thinking about her. At that point, he was with his long-term girlfriend. The girlfriend whom Adolph had just found out that she had lied about something very dear to him. She had actually kept the lie going for almost 8 years.

When it came out, he confronted her, and she eventually caved in. It broke Adolph into pieces. It was something he could not have expected.

Yes, maybe finding out that all the cheating rumours were true or something, that, he would have stomached it better than finding out that he had no blood relation to his only child by then.

This lady just came at the right time. Adolph was convinced that this was a sign that he should move on. He could never trust again so why stay. So, he decided to do just that.

In the weeks that followed, he had seen this woman almost every weekend. On their second meeting, they woke up in the same bed. There were never any discussions about the relationship. It was because like all his other relationships, to him, a relationship was built on synergy. The only way to see that; was to be intimate first. If that department worked out, then he could start talking about a relationship.

At that time, things were cleared out. She was actually not married. She had been engaged and had a child. He was told that they had separated with her ex-husband-to be.

Something should have told him that this would not be real. She had been engaged and has separated with her fiancé while the child was only six months old. So, technically, in a six months period, she had had a husband, had a child, separated with a baby daddy and was then sleeping with a stranger. Adolph had nothing to do with that area. He was just there to get a house, rent it out and go back where he stayed and worked. But there, he was, they were arranging weekends away every weekend.

One morning while they were at a café, Adolph joked that maybe they should get married instead of sneaking behind other people. He did not mean to propose to her at all, but her reaction was something he did not expect.

Adolph could not retract that statement and he did not mind the content of it, but he felt that it was too early to even talk about such things. The next thing they were talking about were rings, about what their families would say etc. They were going to get married. For real. All that happened in just over a month after their meeting. To be exact, it was exactly four weeks. So, she had gotten engaged, had a child, broke up with her baby daddy, met someone else, got engaged again, all within six months. She sure was an over-achiever.

Adolph and Tera got married. It was not a big wedding, but Adolph had fulfilled his side of the ceremony. According to customs, they were married and according to the country's Marriage Laws they were married too.

Finally, Adolph had found what he had been looking for.

………………………..The Reality…………………………

Life was all well. The marriage was going just fine. The child was growing up well. They were in love. Tera had been out of work for almost half a year by then. She had left her job after Adolph had complained that it was stressing her. She would complain about this and that every day. It was not good for her. She was a salesperson. Selling something is a skill. Selling something that most people already have is even a miraculous skill. She was not doing too well. Her manager was not helping. He was one of those guys who held power in their eyes. He was the type who would rather employees run and hide when they see him. To him, that was a sign of how powerful he was. He also had a dark side. Most of the salespersons were women. Most of them were young women from school. This type of a job was a job most people took while waiting for something they needed. It was just a passer-by job. Most of them were desperate. This guy knew that. This manager knew that, so he took advantage of some of them. Adolph was not that type who would allow his then girlfriend to be treated like that. To him, he could afford to give her what she was earning, so he suggested that in order to build a family, she should leave, look for another job or focus on school, so she did.

......................About Tera.........................

Tera was a young and vibrant girl. She was born in a steady family. She only had an older sister. Her parents had long been separated prior to Adolph meeting her. They were divorced to be precise. Her mother had also passed on. Her father had not been part of their life since the divorce.

She was left with her sister and her grandmother and their extended family. She had studied some course at some private college. I must indicate that the clarification that it was a private college is vital.

In our country, there were government, public-private universities and there were these private colleges. Most of the time, people from well developed areas attended these colleges. They offered all the courses that were offered by the traditional universities. However, most of them were not adequately recognized. In essence, in our country, if you wanted to gamble with your career or future, you could easily do that by going to a private college and study a traditional degree.

Traditional degrees in this context were common degrees such as engineering, commerce and medical fields

These degrees were offered at the traditional universities too and those universities were well recognized. The competition in the work environment became high. However, I should indicate that there were courses that these private colleges outshined the traditional universities on.

For an example, courses such as travel and tourism, graphic design, speech and drama, etc. These were what I would call fancy degrees. The private colleges surely outshined the traditional universities on them.

Tera was one of those who attended a private college but did a traditional degree. Her prospect of getting a decent job with that degree was very minimal. That was why she had ended up as a salesperson while she was trying to study something else from a traditional university part-time.

She had enrolled for a course in Law at one of the national universities. Prior to her then current job, she had had some odd jobs before in the human capital management field and the sales and marketing field. She was in her mid-twenties by then.

...................About Adolph.......................

Adolph was one of those people with a fairy tale story. Being raised by a single mother, he had managed to work his way up within the corporate space. He was a Junior Manager at his then current company. He had a couple of sisters and brothers. Some he knew but others he only heard of. He was then studying towards a higher degree. To him, education was everything. He had seen how it had changed his life, so he valued it over most things.

...................The Story.......................

The point was that Adolph had accepted that Tera would not be working. He had tried to convince himself that it was fine. He would be able to take care of her and the child. Throughout the early days, he thought that he was doing fine. This only lasted a very short time. Problems started when he could not figure out what Tera was doing with the money. He would try and calculate her expenses and it would just not make sense.

From the money he was giving her, she used to buy the small things in the house. At some point while Adolph was trying to figure out what was happening, he decided to do the grocery himself for a couple of months. This also did not help. Money was required left and right.

Adolph's pocket was running dry. The tension in the house started getting worse. It was always about one thing, "money". Although Tera may not have understood, but to Adolph, she appeared as if she wasted money. Adolph understood the feeling of poverty, Tera, did not. Their view on spending was miles apart. Adolph believed that living a simple life helps build for the future, while Tera wanted to have whatever she wanted.

It was not always about what she wanted that was the problem. It was about how she wanted it. Adolph could source money whenever he needed to, but things were getting worse.

Adolph had made it clear that he never wanted a housewife.

He would say that "I don't want to marry an expense but rather an asset. Even if I do not get anything from her to grow me, at least I should not be wasting on her". That is what he would say. Wastage to him was not about spending on unnecessary things only but also the fact that he had to take care of the kids and also an adult. In that case he felt that he was then supporting an adult who could support themselves if they had put in some effort. He hated it. He despised it.

The financial issues were piling up. They were just piling up on the basics. Adolph was just a junior manager at work. He was earning fine, but the household expenses were starting to become a problem. Sometimes he would say he hoped that he had found someone from the countryside who would appreciate the life they were living. Unfortunately, Tera was from a different world. She was the so-called previously advantaged people. To her, their then current life was below what she had expected. She was also getting stressed out. Adolph was getting stressed out because he could not offer everything Tera wanted and Tera was stressed out because she felt that she was not pulling her weight around the house.

This started getting worse. Tera was forever stressed. Adolf was forever stressed. The problem with Tera was that when she was upset or stressed, she was very rude. Adolf on the other hand hated people who disrespected him. He knew that anyone can always find a polite way of addressing a problem.

He knew that very well. He was one of the most short-tempered people alive, but he had learned how to deal with it. If he felt in a particular way, he would just keep quiet. So, to him, nothing ever justified Tera's anger outbursts. It was just not justifiable. Sometimes Tera would even…..(it continues on my next book)

…………..Read the rest of it from…………………

The Marriage from Hell
By
Aliana Marshall

THE ~~UN~~MARRIED WIFE

www.ingramcontent.com/pod-product-compliance
Lightning Source LLC
Chambersburg PA
CBHW031301060726
47590CB00003B/1006